CRITICAL MASS

CRITICAL MASS

Kathleen M. Henry

To Rosemarie,
My buddy "left"
on the religious "left" —
out of the box!
Kathleen

iUniverse, Inc.
New York   Bloomington

Critical Mass

This is a work of fiction. All of the characters, names, incidents, organizations, and dialogue in this novel are either the products of the author's imagination or are used fictitiously.

iUniverse books may be ordered through booksellers or by contacting:

iUniverse
1663 Liberty Drive
Bloomington, IN 47403
www.iuniverse.com
1-800-Authors (1-800-288-4677)

ISBN: 978-0-595-52412-9 (pbk)
ISBN: 978-1-4401-0225-7 (cloth)
ISBN: 978-0-595-62466-9 (ebk)

Printed in the United States of America

To Kim, for believing in me

Author's Note

This small volume is the culmination of a dream that began forming in 1976. That dream was to write a fictional piece in which parts of the Mass were intertwined with stories of people's lives. Read no further if a pious and orthodox piece on the Mass is what you think this is. If you are one of the "gentle, angry people," however, read on.

Getting a Handle

1955

✳The dank coolness of the walls would calm her down. The light, dimmed deeply by the glass windows stained with pictures of Mary and Joseph fleeing, of Jesus dying, of Peter standing on his rock, would cool her.

The granite steps were ground down in places to beveled, toothless gums of stairs. Pilgrims and parishioners and beggars and thieves had deepened the furrows in the granite, each approaching the cathedral for everything imaginable, everything both holy and unholy.

On this April day, Anne approached for the cool, for the calm, for the dust motes faintly glowing in the color-stained light as they floated in the ether of the place. And, she wanted to watch him.

The cathedral gripped the side of a hill in a cantilevered kind of way. It was valuable real estate now, but more than a century ago when it was built, this lot would have been the neighborhood with few prospects. The landholding Yankee Episcopalians would never sell property to Catholics to build a church; but if it were merely a lot such as this poor specimen they would. The Mayflower set was determined not to let the Irish Catholics get much of a foothold in the town. The Catholics' church, their *cathedral* as they called it, would indeed not stand on much of a foothold, built as it would have to be on the side of a hill, on a little side street, on a slice- of- pie- shaped lot.

One hundred years after the cornerstone had been laid, Anne O'Brien took the steps slowly, the hill having already winded her. Although her forty-three-year-old frame still seemed fit and still did fit into a respectable size twelve, her forty-three-year-old spirit was exhausted.

She reached for the massive handle. Iron-wrought in a forge, bent and twirled by a master craftsman, this handle was solid enough to last the tugs of thousands of people over the years. It pulled her up the final step. The door loomed; it was thick and heavy, and there was no approach to it. The door met the edge of the stair directly and swung out rather than in, in a way that no modern building code would ever permit . Anne was grateful for the beige cotton spring gloves that she'd found inside her beige purse that morning. She'd brought it out from the back shelf in the closet—a signal that the season was changing. The blacks and browns of winter could be put away and the soft shades of spring could hold sway for fifty or so days until the whites and crisp navies of summertime came out at Memorial Day. Thanks be to God for nice cotton gloves, she thought, as she pulled the big handle on the cathedral's door. *You never know who or what has touched this before you.*

She had to step back and down a bit, out of the door's way, to allow it to open. As she did she felt a queer leap of a fright in her gut that she would tip backward, down the stairs.[1]

---

1. Abby Hoffman could have pulled this door open once. Unlikely, but still possible. John F. Kennedy himself may have stopped by and pulled on it, too. Bishops have definitely stepped through these doors, as well as little Sarah Smiths, hoping for weddings and babies and happiness. The Tommy Hanrahans claimed entry if only for the cool air on a hot day. And Hanrahan the father would come in and cry at the memories of his altar-boy days and of the funeral of his mother oh so many years ago. Pierced-tongued teenagers come here now, their emaciated frames cracking as they pull and pull on the handle of this huge, heavy door. Why do they come? Why does anyone come?

   Women have pulled on this door and others like it, doors that have never opened easily and, in some ways, never opened at all. What's inside doesn't look like "them" or feel like their own. A church of their own would be rounder and lower and deeper, like a kiva. Theirs would be softer in color and texture, and rounder, oh, rounder. It would be a place where all present could hold hands, could dance, could hug and feel equal and free. The flowers inside

You had to be thrown off balance to get into this place.

Anne had meticulously made sure the seams of her nylons, brown wormy strands branding her legs, were straight up the middle of her calves, ready in case anyone in the pews should notice as she walked down the aisle. She thanked God for the miracle of the fabric that was nylon each and every time she gingerly fed her hand, nails carefully wrapped in her balled fist, into the slinky tube. With her other hand, she would gather the mesh with a peeling motion of the thumb as she wended her way down into the darker-colored toe part. Then she would fit the toe part, just that much, onto the top of her foot and slowly, care ... mmm ... carefully unfurl the gathered stocking as she drew it up—smoothing, straightening, smoothing, straightening, around her calf, her knee, her thigh. When clipping the nylon with the metal fastener, she secured the front side first to anchor it and then put her attention to the seam. The challenge was to have it so rightly straight the first time that she only had to clip the back once; readjusting, restraightening, unclipping, and readjusting again would betray a lack of careful preparation..

---

would come from their gardens, the cushions on the pews would come from the work of their hands. The cloths, they would weave them; the prayers, they would write them. The children and old folks would sit side by side. The floors would be flush to the doors as you entered. welcoming wheelchairs and gurneys. You might even be invited to walk through water, to step into a warm, shallow trough as you enter the church so that you would be cleansed and blessed, baptized again and again each time you came.

Instead, the door that the women pull on at Cathedral is huge and massive; it looms. It holds them at bay. It warns, not warms. It is the door of a fortress, not the house of the Spirit. But they come, and pull and pull harder to open the door of the house of the God of their mothers.

They come because she came and her mother before, they come to find solace and glory and, home. Sure this home feels familiar—its silence seems safe though it's run by the men and the rules and the lash. The women are servile and silent, submissive (even all of the cash is collected by men). But it's the women who count it. Oh and the women don't they iron for the altar; oh and the women can sing in the choir. But they can't read the Gospel aloud to those gathered, and cannot presume to say what they think. It doesn't take long for the spell of religion to snap with a crack of disgust and of pain. And it is hard, sure, it really is hard.

It was in her: this practice, this regimen. She treated each stocking as if it were made of silk, and as if it were still 1944 and these hose were the most precious commodity in her possession. She kept her feet soft and smooth, her knees too. The hair on her legs was never a rough stubble. A run was a horror. She repaired runs with needle and thread, creating tiny stitches in webbing so delicate, the needle's point could cause another run if flicked the wrong way. Her repairs were virtually invisible, the very opposite of the ink-brown seams that were considered attractive.

It wasn't so much that life was hard, although it truly was— hard indeed. It was that living required unrelenting vigilance and care.

1910

Molly Donoghue bent over at the waist to fend off the wind and the incline of the hill. She wrapped her shawl more tightly around her shoulders, and the clenched fist that held it to her breastbone betrayed a hard-working thick hand, knuckles ready for arthritis, veins bumpy and blue.

She'd be there in a minute, ah, and all would be well, then, all would be well. Every corpuscle in her sturdy form ached for rest; —stop here, straighten up, take a breath, slow down; —but she did not. She would not rest until she lowered this body into the pew. She would not rest until her fingers crabbed along the string of beads. There would be no resting for her. She would not rest until the Virgin herself looked down upon her from her post on the pedestal to the left of the altar banked with flickering candles that cast the fantasy of warmth. Each flicker was bought and paid for with the pennies of the poor who streamed in to buy a moment of the Virgin's attention, to request her intercession with her son.

It was a cold day even for April. Such a silly month—a hot day on Monday, frozen by Tuesday night. *At least home in Cowskeep, near Waterford on the other side, when the seasons changed, they changed. Or, the fog would warn ye. Or, the moon would have the night before. Here 'twas all so different; there was no telling. Ye bundled up in April and could be like to faint, or, visa versa.*

But Molly had gotten it right this day, As she had pulled out her black wool stockings, she'd wondered. *Put these on*, she'd thought, *and you are ensuring blistering heat will be the weather. God who shapes the stars and moon is planning his day and sure if he sees you chose wool stockings, he'll raise the sun's shining to a hotter pitch. Wait and see.*

But it wasn't so. It was cool and stayed cool. And they had felt good all day, her black stockings. Itching of course, but a layer of protection against the wind. They were clean, just two days of wearing so far, and the newly mended patch at the back of her right heel was a smooth darning job, without a lump. As she'd pulled them up, the skin on her legs had flaked off like soap shavings, patches of dry from the winter so soon to go. The wool rubbed against her fair skin and scratched it to raw behind her knees, between her thighs. But she was warm. and she owned two pair of these strong stockings that would last her through. Each evening, she eyed them carefully for signs of wear, her needle and darning egg at the ready. They too would last her through.

Life was hard, truly hard. But she had her own room with a lamp, she had a needle and thread and a darning egg, and she was free—free to pay attention to these personal matters with vigilance and care.

Molly's right hand, cracked from water and bleach, and sore anyway from what all, reached for the big handle on the cathedral door. As she stretched her fingers to fit around its curve, she winced. In fact, she hung onto it a bit, letting it take her weight, letting it hold her up, her shoulders sinking into laxness for just a minute. Just for a minute.

Ooh! She blinked, for indeed, the resting hurt too. Up and out she tugged, pulling on the handle and stepping down and back out of the door's way. Then she pushed her shoulder around and nudged it onto the inside of the door to hold it back, so she could make her legs, one at a time, move up and over the threshold.

With her body bent and swathed as it was in the shawl, with the heavy wool of her stockings, with her long skirt and patched petticoat, she could have been a laborer stooped over tubers in some potato field. She had to steady herself to stand up straight, her hand out, palm flat against the doorframe as the door shut hard behind her, pushing her forward a stumbling step. But, ah, the smell of the beeswax candles, the lingering scent of the burnt wicks now snuffed. These were the same smells the world over. This could be the tiny church in Cowskeep, the smells were so much the same. To Molly, the smells were what made it the Church Universal.

1998

Christine didn't care who saw her trudging up the hill to the cathedral. Told herself that all the while wondering who might be watching and judging her to be some loony, pious sycophant. Or worse, a hypocrite; agnostic one minute and in the pew the next.

As she stopped and adjusted her fold-up umbrella, she noticed the backs of her pantyhose were soaked, and the dye from her sopping shoes was beginning to stain her feet navy blue.

"They call this April showers?"

The lever on the umbrella stabbed her thumb. "Ow!" she managed, quite out loud. "*And anyway,*" she carried on the interior argument, "*underwear is irrelevant. Spend good money for underpants that won't show a panty line through your slacks, good money, extra expensive underpants that make it look like you are not wearing underpants. Shit. Forget the fucking underpants and give that money to the ones who don't have enough to buy underpants.*"

Not that she didn't have on underpants. This ongoing theoretical argument inside her head was her Herzognian letter to the editor about society, culture, current events, and the second coming of Jesus H. Christ, for God's sake, that she waged on and on, on the bus, in the shower, or at her desk, waiting for the Internet to dial and connect. Her rumbling hum of discontented analysis (how hard, stupid, really meaningless and irrelevant life was, goddamnit) gummed up Christine like a viscous membrane.

As soon as she reached up for the handle on the cathedral door Christine Roy was hit with the fact that she'd lost another fingernail tip; another eight-fifty for two cents' worth of silicone and glue down the drain. Once you'd committed to nails you had to keep them up or it looked ridiculously shabby and adolescent. But finding the time to sit still for a professional to do the repair was impossible. The god-awful fumes and the crackling voices of the Vietnamese ladies and the blaring of their Vietnamese MTV made it all just not worth it.

As she pulled open the cathedral door, it flipped her backward a bit, and she felt another nail bend. It didn't break, but it did hurt, and all of it was infuriating. She reached for the holy water font just to the right of the door in the vestibule, as much to grip its strong marble for support as to dip in for the blessing. There used to be sponges in the wells of these things, she remembered from when she was a little girl. Germ-infested, no doubt about it.

"In the name of the … " she began to sweep of the sign of the cross over her chest with her dampened third and fourth fingers, as if hypnotized, then stopped.

"In the name of the … " *Stop. Breathe. Slow it down. Do not rush through this as if nothing mattered.* Maybe *something matters. Maybe it isn't this particular act that has meaning, but maybe just the intention itself. Slow it down.*

"In the name of the … Holy One," she prayed, putting her hand to her forehead as if to soothe a headache. Then she prayed, "Let something matter. Something …."

Entrance Procession

[The congregation stands as the priest enters the sanctuary.]

✳ *Like hell.* Molly Donoghue was there for the Virgin Mary and not for any priest so she would not stand. It was indeed a mortal sin to absent yourself from Mass, but there was nothing, not a thing, in any of the teachings she'd ever heard that could make her stand up just because the priest was coming in. None of them had ever stood up for her or hers, in a manner of speaking, and she'd be damned if they'd get her to stand up for one of them, any of them. Her face as collected and serene as a statue of the Madonna herself, Molly Donoghue never removed her gaze from the Virgin's altar when the bells at the sacristy door were rung to signal the beginning of the Mass and the entrance of the celebrant.

[All stand.]

She dangled her rosary from her right hand and thumbed the beads in the soft circling murmurs that her thumb and forefinger and third finger made, in the tiny ebbs and rhythms of circles. Georgie had held her hand like that once. Up behind the house. They had sat there until the stars came out just for them. He'd held her hand and moved his thumb in gentle circles over and over and over the width and the length of her thumb. Nothing else. Not even words. They sat and watched the stars as the universe drew back its curtain, revealing sparkles and mystery and caverns of speed and stillness.

She held her rosary with her right hand and kneaded the beads, fingering them through the prayers. As she leaned her left elbows on the pew in front of her, her left hand alternately cradled her forehead or unfolded itself flat and jarringly real over her heart, her eyes fast on the

Virgin, in an almost Italianate way of praying, which she had long ago adopted not realizing it seemed out of character for an Irish immigrant woman to show such emotion.

Her hand was over her heart, however, to keep her from crying, from crying aloud. She was holding the emotion in tightly, and that fit the Irish immigrant woman. *Remember, oh most gracious Virgin Mary, never was it known that anyone who fled to thy protection, implored thy help, or sought thy intercession was left unaided.*

Others might hold their beads in both hands, securely, cleanly finishing off with one Hail Mary before beginning the next, designating which mystery the decade was honoring, demarcating beginnings and middles and ends. To such as they, Molly's hold would have appeared casual, sloppy. But it was not carelessness that left her beads to dangle precariously from her hand; it was indeed her one last desperate grip no matter how weak, a fevered memorized incantation that alone kept the prayer flowing. The prayer prayed itself. Molly was barely there; her tenuous connection to the prayer, to the beads, now as involuntary as breathing, was what kept her sane.

Praying the rosary had not been about belief for a very long time, not since Georgie. It was about sanity. Molly Donoghue was barely holding on.

Anne knew she was being perfect. When the entrance bell rang, she "jumped to." Really, she was on her feet even before the bell rang. At the instant Father Michael flicked the cord that would swing the bell and send the clapper ringing, at the instant before the sound had *begun* let alone traveled, at that instant, as if the flick of his wrist had triggered her, upright she went. Perfect. Always, too, the flicker within her: *Does he notice how quickly I stand, how silently, how seemingly calmly, how straight, how poised, how prayerful, pious? How pious, how perfect I am?*

Her shoulder-length chapel veil draped in fluid folds. She always wore a black one. Other colors were making their way into fashion (baby blues and lavenders, fuchsias even, to match or coordinate with Sunday-best suits), but a black chapel veil would always symbolize piety over fashion, and she certainly wanted that to be her image. On feast days of Mary, however, she switched to a pure white veil. It was important that she did so because it indicated her observance of feast days, her respect for the Virgin, and that her choice was a conscious one to wear what she was wearing, so as not to give the appearance of always donning a black chapel veil out of mere habit.[2]

---

2. Anne had wanted to be a sacristan so badly it was an ache. How would she ever get them to even notice her, let alone allow her? She was public, after all, and couldn't be counted on for piety or good training.

It was only ever the parochial school girls who were picked to be sacristans. It was an honor above all others for a girl. The nun in charge of the sacristy washed all the altar linens each week, bleached them brilliant, tortured her hands with the soap and the scrubbing and the bleach and the starch. The ironing went on for hours. The iron had to be very, very, very hot because the altar cloths were Irish linen, and the ironer had to be very skilled so as not to leave a scorch. These linens were blessed, which made them sacramentals, as the nuns' habits were, and therefore, washing and ironing them earned you indulgences—a Monopoly pass-jail kind of saving grace that cut short your stay in purgatory.

The high school girls from Our Lady of the Angels who were sacristans got to carry the linens to their specially sized drawers in the sacristy, the room off the sanctuary where the priest dressed in his vestments for Mass. They also got to polish the ciborium and the paten and the chalice. They got to set foot on the floor of the sanctuary where the altar stood. The only women who had that privilege were sacristans, except for a bride on her wedding day when her *pris dieu* was located on the sanctuary side of the communion rail which showed how important the sacrament of marriage was. The girls were trained just how and when to genuflect or instead bow as they crossed back and forth in front of the tabernacle, sweeping the carpet and adjusting the dressings of the season.

Anne's place in this all came about because of Father Lahey.

Father Lahey was a *cure' d'Ars*, a holy and humble man with a shaggy head of white hair and random whiskers that grew out from his saggy neck, which spilled out above the priestly collar. He was stooped, a great hump on his back like a turkey breast ready for carving. He wore a cassock all the time—the long black dress swished around his trousers as he walked. So threadbare were the soles of his shoes that sometimes a titter would circulate in the congregation when he knelt facing the altar, his back to the people, to say the *Introibo Ad Altare Dei*. People would give him money for new shoes. He would give it away. People would give him new shoes. He would give them away.

His stoop twisted him into a posture where he was always looking up to whomever he was speaking, even fifteen-year-old

Sometimes Christine was the only one in the congregation—that she could see at least—who turned toward the center aisle as the priest entered in procession from the back of the church. In the old days, he and the altar boys just slipped in from the sacristy off to the side of the altar. Since all the changes, though, the priest entered from the back. Christine assumed it was to symbolize—better said, give the appearance—that the priest actually "came from the people." Not that he did come from them in any appreciable way once he'd been seminarianized and ordainitized and hierarchicized, but it was a sweet symbol.

So, she forcefully turned to face the center aisle to welcome him, as it were, to "her" Mass, to the Mass the congregation had invited him, indeed ordained him, to celebrate for them. She did so as if the attempted symbolism *were* the truth and not the myth she knew it to be.

She was full of awareness about the true meaning behind rituals and symbols. What she was not full of was confidence that her fellow congregants had any clue about what was really going on in "their" church, either politically or theologically. What she was full of was contempt—she would have said contempt for the institution, but the subject of her loathing was much more venal that that. Yes, she bore disdain for the priests who were throttled by the golden collars of power and prestige, and by the inner circle of fraternity that plumped them up. But she bore a disdain close to hatred for the Catholics in the pew, who thought nary a twit of a thought about such incongruities as the, quote, infallibility of the pope, unquote, but simply believed whatever it was expected of them to believe in a *table la rasa* way. Their Bible might as well still be chained to the walls of the church. They needed only a gesture from the priest to reckon how they would believe. The ones she despised the most were the radical feminists, as

---

then Anne Cooney who wasn't very tall at all. He was aware she came every day to pay a visit, and he wondered in a gentle, amused way if she thought she would be a nun. On this day, he noted that her shoulders were heaving as if she were crying. And, indeed, Anne Cooney was crying, kneeling there, paying her visit to the Blessed Sacrament.

"What is it, girl?" He came up near to her in the pew just in front of where she knelt. "What is it then?" Anne thought the kindness in his eyes could soothe any ache there was, forgive any sin. "I, I—" Anne couldn't quite catch her breath. "I want to be a sacristan, but I'm public." And on "public" she wailed. "There, there, my dear. There, there." He patted her on the shoulder.

they called themselves, who yet claimed this church as their own and still held positions on parish councils and in parish schools, while all the time holding intemperate and largely silent opinions about women's ordination and choice.

Christine herself had no delusions. She knew this church was not *her* church. It was this God that was her God and that was why she came—although sometimes she even wondered if that were true.

[All stand.]

Her shoulders squared off, she faced the center aisle and looked over at the people in the pew across who stared straight ahead at the altar, their backs to the priest as he came down the aisle—*as if he were the enemy*, she thought, *but then he'd be making a surprise attack on these numb folk*. Then, *no,* she realized with a cluster burst of insight, *they are not displaying disrespect to the priest; instead, they're just showing how subjugated they are to him. I will look him in the eye*, she thought. *I will look him in the eye.*

[All stand.]

A religious sister was in position in the pew just behind the students. Sister Mary Perpetua's attendance at Mass in the church was distinctly different from her normal attendance in the convent chapel. She was not devotional in the least in church; she was vigilance personified. Her eyes rarely took in the priest or the servers and certainly never any of the others in the congregation. Her duty was to monitor her charges to ensure the training she provided them in catechism class was indeed sticking.

Once a month, for the Children's Mass at 9:00 AM, and, of course, once a year for First Holy Communion, Sister Mary Perpetua took her usual sentry post in the eighth pew on the left side on the edge of the center aisle. She had decided to consider it a huge promotion for Michael John, her brother, to be stationed at the cathedral after only two years at Holy

---

It would take some doing, he knew. It was Ambrose herself who oversaw Sacristy and who specially trained her OLA students in the rules and the rubrics. It would take some doing, but he would get it done, and Anne would be a sacristan.

To mark the beginning of her four-year tenure, working her way up to head sacristan, Anne sewed a small purse out of black satin, with a glass button, to hold her chapel veil. She had to always be at the ready to enter the sanctuary, and a female could never do so without a head covering. She folded her veil neatly and slipped it into its satchel, which she then slid into the pocket of her public school jacket. At the ready. Always.

Redeemer. She attributed her being able to affect her own transfer to the Mercy convent at the cathedral to her deceased mother's miraculous intervention, to her own total abstinence from asking anything else of her superiors at any time except this one huge favor, and to the wisdom of the bishop who had begun to understand that she was indeed an influence for stability and good over her brother.

Nuns moved in July, priests in August; being moved in April was unheard of. There was some anguish and much analysis in her mind about her brother's transfer because although it was indeed an honor to be stationed at the cathedral, he would no longer pastor his own parish as he had at Holy Redeemer. Rather, he would fill that nebulous position of associate. Did that mean the bishop was losing confidence in Michael John? Or, on the contrary, did it point to bigger and better things ahead? Was he being groomed to become the pastor of the cathedral? Oh, he needed work on the social obligations that such a post would involve—which invitations to accept and which to decline. The fancy donors who'd removed to the suburbs still contributed masses of money to the diocese's primary church, its cathedral, and those people needed soliciting and thanking and attention. He was only scarcely paying attention to *her*. How would she succeed in training him for the hospitality circuit in store for him? If he would only play golf, that would take care of so much.

How she knew all these things was from the movies she'd seen as a child and from reading, especially *Life* magazine. It *was* life they taught you when you read that magazine.

The Sign of the Cross

(In nomine patris)

ACT I: Silver and Gray

SCE

(Black and white phc
Christine stands in h
begins the motions of
cross. Right hand swe

CHRI

✳It is only in "a way" that I remer
it is actually just a photograph of
picture of two strangers whom I v
and myself around fifteen months
father's, younger and more vital tha
and it must be I who is the toddler, ᵣᵢₛ ₗₐₛₜ ₑₕᵢₗₔ.

He leans on his elbow against a grassy slope. He wears an undershirt—the immigrant thin kind—ribbed, its straps narrow and armholes loose, used. For him to appear outdoors dressed like this, it must very, very hot, and he must be very, very young. Later, dignity will overtake him like a moss.

I am in a sundress, all ruffles. My shoes are white leather tie shoes with necks for strengthening my ankles. It was believed you learned to walk better with good shoes. Buy them good shoes when they are babies and you save them from a future of misery.

In the memory, which is really a photograph, there are no colors to anything, just shades of white and gray and silver.

I am glee. My whole little pudgy body is joy. I run downhill away from my daddy as if into the arms of the camera. His smile leaps off his face into the air in front of him, following me with paramount attention as I toddle, as I run, all giggles and dimples. His rimless glasses spark a hint of the sunlight, marking their shape and their texture. The size of coins, they are crystal over his eyes, coins of crystal pressed over his eyes. Coins pressed over his eyes.

> (Christine bends and motions as if closing the eyes of someone lying directly in front of her.)

He is taking delight in me. He watches me skip away from him, toward the world. He lets me run. He sets me free. He delights in my joy, my freedom. And he is inside my freedom, somehow, and he runs with me. He partakes.

> (Christine brings her hands together in prayer, a gesture of Amen.)

I see the photograph and I know that when my daddy was a new daddy he loved me beyond measure, and I see in the eye of my mind his ecstasy. I see it in silvers and grays and tones of white. I see it framed and crisp and clear. Proof. Documented proof. Amen.

Prayers before the Altar

Introibo ad altari dei (I will go up to the altar of God)

✳Saturday afternoons, three o'clock to four. Damp dust, dark daylight, and memories of dark daylight. Linoleum floor waxes, "weary but keeping up" smells. Masses in the lower church, shuffles, cracking kneelers. Confessionals proofed from being overheard by motionless velvet drapes, thick and not yet moth-eaten, still emerald green and falling, falling in folds.

Inside, so hot, so cramped. Some are scared to go in. Some go out of pity for the priest, so ancient and ravenous a scavenger.

There, by the altar perpetually burning, the red light in the glass, the light in the red glass. There, images threaten to snuff you. Flat, whole-eyed icons chained and framed.

There, the penance you pray before the altar of God permits you to receive the next day.

Sunday, slipped under and waiting, the man in the gown moves slowly, the throngs kneel and bow and bend.

Catch it if it falls. But do so with the paten, the plate, for it is golden enough, enough to hold it, purer than we, than our hands. If it were loaves and fish instead of bread and wine, would the bones turn into God? And the skin? And the eyes?

The priest inexorably moves, whispering *Corpus Domini nostri Jesu Christi custodiat animam tuam in vitam aeternam,* moving down, down the line, to a rhythm of

Dip to cup
Show the host
Place on tongue
Step to next
Dip
To cup
Show
The host
Place
On tongue
Step to the next
Cup
Host
Tongue
Step
Cup
Host
Tongue
Step
Corpus animam tuam
Step to the next
In vitam aeternam
Step to the next.
Amen.

Kyrie

ACT II: Have Mercy

SCENE I

(Spot up on a priest on a platform raised above the stage. In the background, a liturgical Kyrie is being chanted. He removes his long black cape and then his long black cassock and then his collar and shirt, and then his black trousers. He is wearing conservative white boxer shorts. He removes them and puts on tight jockey underpants, then puts the boxers on over them, then puts on the black trousers, the cassock, the collar, the cape, then, a beretta on his head. Over it all, he puts on a vestment for Mass, stiff as if waxed, like an insect's shell. Spot out. Spot up on a woman, legs crossed, smoking a cigarette.)

SMOKING WOMAN:

✳If he could have been what he really was, it would probably have been gay. Probably.
    (Pause while she inhales deeply.)

    Had he been an Episcopalian priest instead of the Roman variety and had he been born thirty years later, the Episcopalian diocese would have rewarded him with an elevation to bishop. Probably.

(Crosses and recrosses her legs, and tugs on her short skirt firmly.)

I danced with him once at a big summer party. All of us kids from the parish had been invited to a party in his parents' backyard.

(Spot out on Smoking Woman. We continue to hear her voice.)

The air smelled of breeze itself and of the roses his father grew. The house imposed itself upon a hill, its front banking quilted with row after row of his father's prize rose bushes. The plantings rendered the landscape ugly for many months of barrenness but gave way finally and briefly to a lush tangle of magentas and pinks and scarlets, a bright bedspread on a summer's afternoon, tossed and rumpled and catching the western light.

Their backyard was cool, dark, shaded to almost grim by tall, leafy plants and arbors. The front side of the house blared color and sunlight, but in the backyard you had to pull on a sweater even on an afternoon in July.

At the party, long tables with bowls of salads, slaws, and beans were set up near the back door of the house, accessible to the kitchen. His mother had covered the tables with paper cloths and had set up matching pastel napkins in a pattern of folded triangles, as if this were a garden party, a tea, and we were her social set. The boys in our group had been visitors here occasionally before, but never the whole group like this, girls and boys, with parent advisors, too. Our church was in the city and our families were generally not as well-to-do as his family. Hanging in the air was our unspoken fear that one of us would do something embarrassing.

(Spot on Smoking Woman. She stands and does a turn around her chair.)

SMOKING WOMAN:

We danced—he and I—to "Henry the Eighth, I Am."

(Spot moves with her like a dancing partner. She does not speak aloud, but we hear her.)

He'd abandoned his official garb for shorts and a polo shirt. And his face, flushed from the dancing at least if not also from the adventure of mixing his two worlds, popped with excitement. He was not being sardonic for once and, because of that, I had a sense he was real in that moment instead of someone manufactured and protected by Rome and his mother. Who is to say which image was the real one, however? He said to me as we jumped up and down in the silly dance the song called for, "If my mother catches sight of me doing this, she will kill me." And we laughed, "I am, I am," mouthing the words, we danced, conspirators delighting in the rhythm. I was delighted that he, this priest, the authority, could joke that he was still subject to his mother's dismay. The reference to disappointing mother, our common condition, shot me full of pride that I was being chosen (for this brief measure of time as his confidant).

> (She sits and lights another cigarette.
> She continues,conspirator-ially, almost gossipy now.)

His best friend from high school, Jim, had become a priest too, and he was there at the party as well as MaryAnne, the girl they each had dated way back when. She was a fifties paradigm in her pastel cotton shirtwaist dress, with a matching headband threading through her shoulder length Breck-blonde hair. The sixties were happening, but she was still old-school, serving punch and cold potato salad, surrounded by the two young men she had lost to Christ's service, assisting the mother of her old boyfriend.

We were not at all surprised that she was there. And we were not at all surprised as the story of their dating spread in hushed murmurings among us, as we danced and sipped cold cola. We knew she had been invited so that we girls could admire her. She was the model of sacrifice and chastity. Look what she had given up for God: both of them handsome, young, virile, smart, funny, sociable. She had lost twice. I remember wondering what was wrong with her.

Had his mother called her to say, "We're going to throw a party for Father Billy and the kids from his parish and invite Jimmy, um, Father Jimmy, too. Like the parties we used to have for you young people when you all were their age. Hot dogs, punch. Come, MaryAnne, dear, it will be such fun." Then, had she opted to attend because it was a chance to see him? Or, a chance to be seen as the good girl, to be remembered as always happy to help out?

Her shoulders bowed slightly, drawn forward as if to block her breasts from view, protect them. Her shoulder blades stuck out as if her back were growing the breasts. In her middle age, she would develop the high, rounded ellipse of a stomach that would look like a tumor, her legs would thin out even more to sticks, and her fingers would be chapped from paperwork in an office somewhere. Blondes fade.

I couldn't bring myself to actually talk to her. At one point, I approached the table and leaned in for a paper cup of Jell-O-colored punch, but I did not even look over the punch bowl at her. I scooped up the drink with a little bow of my head, noting as I did how she must have freshly ironed her shirtwaist dress before arriving, because the pleats at the belt were sharp and there were no horizontal wrinkling lines (indicating she had not sat down for long).

She wore a charm bracelet, sterling silver, each link filled. I couldn't see the shoes she had on, but she probably had stockings and skimmers—those ones that looked like ballet slippers. Probably. Even though it was summer and most of us had on shorts and sandals and bare, bare legs. I wished a nun's "religious vocation" for her, in which her single life, her losses, would be indemnified by her vows of chastity, obedience, and poverty. Indemnified by sanctifying grace and heavenly purpose.

As I jumped the dancing steps to the Dave Clark Five and the Beatles, I calculated my situation, my ranking, versus hers—I, fifteen years her junior. I thought about how much smarter I would be about my future. For certain, no one would be able to say that any man had chosen the priesthood over me, and even more for certain, I would not stick around my hometown long enough to be doing tea-party service for the mother-in-law I couldn't close the deal on.

"Gotta' go," he waved and hopped off, still dancing.

I turned and picked up the beat with the kids next to me. "I am, I am."

It was years before I realized it was Jim to whom he was drawn and not MaryAnne, years more before it dawned on me what a temptation the boys in our youth group must have presented to him. More than temptation. Probably.

(Spot on priest, he is dressed in shorts and a sport shirt. MaryAnne stands next to him in the shirtwaist dress, the skimmer shoes, the ribbon holding back her hair. They face the audience and move forward to crowd the footlights. Smoking Woman stands with them.)

SMOKING WOMAN:

He stands here now, MaryAnne too, at the edge where the footlights trick you into forgetting there are actually people in the audience. Both of them scream, their hands in their hair.

PRIEST, MARYANNE, SMOKING WOMAN:

Stop it. Stop it. You cannot know how it was, what temptations were, what vocations were. You cannot know how any of it was. For mercy's sake, stop it. Stop it.

Gloria

Gloria in eggshellcis[3] deo

✳Irishmen who had money at the turn of the century mostly from importing fine whiskeys and who turned their businesses into a more clandestine type of importing during the 1920s in America, upon their deaths, often left their mansions in the country to orders of nuns.

The sisters of Mercy had several of these mansions. One was used as a rest home for the elderly sisters, another for the motherhouse—the seat of the order—where the mother general resided and to which the entire congregation of sisters returned for wakes and funerals, congregation-wide meetings, and special feast days.

The novitiate was a beautiful Victorian unseen from the street in a woody part of a quiet town outside Worcester, called Grafton. This house had originally been built by Yankee money that had been made in the manufacturing of yarn. The last son had scandalized the family by marrying a Catholic girl who outlived him and left the rambling twenty-bedroom-or-more-house to the sisters of Mercy. The sisters had seen her through school. The very thought of the Yankee forebears who had built those walls looking down from heaven (or ... *not*) to witness their palace invaded by papists was the source of some humor among the sisters.

---

3. "Pronounce it as if it you were saying *egg shells*, dear girls. Egg shells. That way it comes out right and everyone in church will know what you're saying, dear girls. Egg shells."

Because it was both an historic building and a novitiate, some concessions were made by the sisters in charge to preserve its original beauty, while still teaching the vow of poverty and a humble, luxury-free life. For instance, the mirrors, one in almost every room, each more ornate and beautiful than the last, were not taken down but simply covered with black cloth. Sisters of Mercy were not allowed to look at their reflections, ever, lest they be tempted to commit the sin of vanity.

Most girls were escorted by their parents on the day they entered. Embraces and kisses, promises to pray and to write happened in small clusters across the broad front lawn and on the curving drive. Brigid Connors arrived by cab, alone. The mistress of novices observed her as Brigid quickly peeled off dollar bills from a wad she then stuffed back into her jacket. Brigid then nodded to the cabbie and swooped her one valise up in a sprightly swing. Happiness had filled her body the whole ride out from Worcester, until it was overflowing. She was here; she was home. Her mother, safely ensconced now in the state hospital for the mentally ill, would not require her services any longer. She was free. And in her freedom she chose this life of obedience and chastity and poverty. She spun around and almost knocked the novice mistress backward off her feet. "Oh, Sister Mary Clemens, I am so sorry, please forgive me, I...."

"That is quite all right, Miss Connors. Please settle down now. It is almost time."

"Oh, and here, Sister," Brigid handed the wad of money over to Clemens. "I'll be having no need of this from now on."

"No, indeed." Sister Mary Clemens was not impressed at the surrender of the illicit cash because there would never have been an opportunity for the silly girl to spend it anyway. But she had done the right thing, that was true, something worth taking into account. Silly girl.

The girls more or less lined up, the forty-two of them, like children in the schoolyard waiting for the opening bell. Sister Mary Clemens stood on the porch at the top of the steps saying nothing at all. She flicked the wrist of her right hand in just a way to communicate "move" and "now." And they filed past her into the novitiate with no time to turn for one last look.

They were led first to the presses, a great bank of oak cabinet doors, floor to ceiling, that housed the habits and accoutrements of nun-clothes. The postulants were each handed two white long-sleeved, high-necked blouses and one gray gabardine jumper, two pair of dark gray cotton hose, and seven pair of white cotton bloomers and three heavy white undershirts. They had each been required to purchase their shoes before coming (black oxfords with laces and fat two-inch heels). They would be instructed in the days to come as to how to launder and care for their habits and shoes. They would also be instructed how to sew from scratch their "real" habits, black with a white veil for the second year, which was the novice year, and then black with a black veil for the rest of their lives.

It was clear that several of the young women, eighteen to twenty-one, most of them, were scared; sniffles punctuated Sr. M. Clemens' remarks. The savvy among them knew full well that someone would no doubt leave before tomorrow night's supper.

Brigid Connors took the carefully folded pile of clothing in her arms as if it were an award, the flag handed to the widow at the veteran's grave, precious and serious. She could barely wait to exchange her suit of business and the world for the clothes that were a prayer just putting them on. She had remembered to take off her rouge. Deep breath. Deep breath.

Later, pausing, indulging yourself in a long, thick gaze at the full moon when all she were supposed to do was empty the garbage in the back of the carriage house was probably not allowed. Her first supper in community done, her assignment was to help the sister in the kitchen with clean up. The luminescence of the moon bathed the grounds in light, a light almost snowy. She could feel it on her body as if it were touching her instead of shining on her. Slowly, slowly she walked the flagstone path back to the kitchen. She cast one final quick moon-look that would have to last her, and thought with a shiver: no wonder the pagans worshipped the moon. They would dance in a light such as this. They would sing.

Brigid prayed, then, to the glory of God in this world of his creation, in this universe of planets and stars so vast and of God so much more vast. Give glory to God. Deep breath. Deep breath.

"Long time that took you, dear girl." Sister Mary Angeline, the cook, dug deep into the pot she was washing, its lip cutting in at her underarm. "Be careful, now, dear girl, be careful. Lollygagging is frowned upon here as you can well imagine. Work to be done. Respect for your superiors and for the other postulants means pulling your own weight, dear girl. Lollygagging is coasting now, isn't it?"

Brigid bowed a little curtsey, almost a genuflection, in silence, for the postulants were not allowed to speak unless told to by the mistress. Then she nodded in a thank-you and left for her next task. Evening prayer would be in fifteen minutes and she was to straighten up the hymnals in the chapel. She would pull her own weight.

She would be given the name Mary Ambrose, an auspicious name—a father-of-the-church name—surely that indicated they had high hopes for her.

> (The scene changes; it is many years later. Mother General Sister Mary Ambrose and several sisters file onto what looks to be a porch. They are now on retreat and so are particularly subdued. The porch on which they stand looks over the bay and the only light is the full moon. A telescope is positioned centrally on the porch. It tantalizes them. Finally, Mother General Ambrose speaks.)

AMBROSE:

I don't see why anyone would mind if we took a look through this thing. It must be here for that purpose.

> (The sisters nod and quietly giggle and set about adjusting their veils and their coifs and their gamps so that they may be able to get close enough to the eye cup of the spyglass. One turn after another, each steps back and gasps in stark amazement. We hear a voice speaking, but the sisters do not. Perhaps Mother Ambrose does.)

THE VOICE:

Life proceeds. Nature breathes in and out for us. Chives grow wild. Rain gathers itself in fissures and caverns. Osprey mothers scream their warnings, and starfish may not know a world exists beyond their tidal pool. We do not at all feel a part of it. We observe with great care from a distance of many paces through a glass ground to precise specifications. Yes, we feel blessed by the bounty of the natural world. Yes, we experience its beauty and some hint of its power but until we know that we, too, are observed and marveled at by some greater intelligence, we will not feel at all a part of it, just superior to it.

Will it be God whom we acknowledge as the greater observer? Or, will it be the dead? Or, the unborn? Whom will we say watches us, sees us grow wild, hears our screams of warning?

The telescope reaches us the moon. "Reach me a rose, Gatsby, from that there crystal vase." Reach me the moon.

Craters the size of thumbprints pitch themselves to us, sisters, through the telescope, and we are shocked at the clarity of the rims of those craters. Shocked.

Each of us gasps, one and then another and another as each of us steps to the viewing eye, to wince her face to capture the focus. Even after having assured herself that she would not gasp as the others had, that this time, this one sister would step up to the telescope, peer through its lens, and hold inside any shock or amazement she might feel steaming up, she-- as each of us one after the other--gasps, not being able to help it. We are shocked at the pock-marked face of the moon, so close, so clear, so real.

> (All sisters have had a turn viewing. They step forward to stand side by side in a line along the edge of the porch, stage forward, crowding the footlights. They look at the assembly, their backs to the moon. The mother general speaks.)

AMBROSE:

For this moment, in the dark, at the edge of the porch, at the edge of the sea, we know we live on the surface of a planet. As it hangs and spins in space, so do we, oblivious to the motion beneath the feet we stand on, shocked at the nearness of the moon.

Epistle

(This is a letter)

✳In those days, a Catholic church would have no sign on its front lawn—especially not the black, felty, grid kind the Protestant churches all had, with movable lettering that said some such about welcoming you. Protestant churches welcomed people; Catholic churches did not, because it was assumed that you knew if you belonged, and if you didn't know, you didn't belong. The primary indicator of the Catholicity of a given church, however, was the cross on top of the steeple. Such icons were considered by Protestants to be showy at best, even idolatrous, so their church steeples just pointed blankly toward the heavens without any brand, any marker to show the way.

Holy Redeemer did not look exactly Catholic. While it had no felty sign out front and it did have the steeply cross, Holy Redeemer could have been taken for Episcopal because it was wooden, painted brown with yellowed ivory trim, and shingled. It was a structure that was a worry when the Easter candle was lit, or when the eight-year-old altar boys who shouldn't be playing around with matches anyway started the incense from the charcoal in the sacristy. Oh, and it had only a middle aisle, no side aisles, no escape routes. The pews bled right up to the side walls under the stations of the cross, so if the farthest person into the pew had some height and should stand up too quickly at the Gospel, say, sure that person could knock a forehead right into the foot of Jesus Falls the Second Time.

It was Father Michael John O'Sullivan who pastored the people of Holy Redeemer. He was the younger brother—blood brother, that is—to Sister Mary Perpetua. Perpetua, a sister of Mercy, was also stationed at Redeemer's, at the convent, a highly unusual, almost to say incestuous, personnel arrangement that her mother general took great exception to but which the bishop himself seemed to have no problem with at all. Perpetua, a reedy woman, was so dry her lips caught hold on her teeth. She had to run her tongue, darting, quick over them, to get her lips apart to smile or to speak. Perpetua was the nun who taught all of the little ones everything they needed to know in the First Holy Communion catechism class. *Introibo ad altare Dei* … I will go up to the altar of God, the God who gives joy to my youth.

When she was thirteen, Sister Mary Perpetua—Josephine then— took hold of her dying mother's already cold hand (oh, and her mother dying at only forty-one) and promised her that she would always look after her brother, Michael John. No matter what. Her mother left her a letter too. "Look after him" was all it said.

When her brother heard the call to priesthood, Josephine entered the convent, a local order called the Mercies that would ensure she would not be missioned out to foreign lands. So she could be close to him always. He did not know how to cook or clean or clothe himself, but of course there would always be housekeepers to perform those duties for a priest. What mother had meant and what Josephine—Perpetua— had agreed to, was guardianship.

There was nothing that escaped her notion or her intuition. Once when he'd been a mere curate, he'd announced to her that he wanted to go to Cape Cod for a two-week summer vacation alone, instead of with his brotherpriests. She told him he was to wear his blacks the whole time and that if he ever purchased a sports coat, a "blazer," with money earned as a priest, he would be committing a sin against his vow of celibacy no matter what happened while he was wearing it. *Thou art a priest forever according to the order of Melchizadec,* she reminded him, and that meant even on vacation. Nuns, on the other hand, were never on vacation. Nuns only got to go on thirty-day directed retreats in houses near seashores, where they remained grand-silenced and habited and hotter than hell, imprisoned in black gabardine ten feet from the surf. That was a vacation for a Mercy. If he ever bought a tie she would know it, just know it, she would feel, smell, his sinfulness like some seeping perspiration. Of that he needed no reminding. She'd expect a postcard. He would oblige.

Drinking, however, was allowed, and he did a lot of drinking.

Fraternizing with the girls in the Holy Redeemer Youth Club was not in the realm of possibility, of course, but it was only the girls in the parish who were at all interesting. They had interior lives; they read books and whispered agonized confessions of masturbating and letting petting go too far. Michael John believed it was their anguish that affected him so. How sensitive they were. How pure they were in their wishes, at least, if not always in their carnal behaviors. The boys were lummoxes, interested only in scores both on the field and off. He wanted to be with the girls, to talk with them, to smell their hair, but it was only safe to be friends with the boys. The boys could even come up to his room and watch sports on television. They would take rides in the car—always a bunch of them—and they would stop for ice cream at some far out country dairy. He'd drop them off back at their homes, wave to the parents, and drive away feeling a loneliness so thorough, so hollow, that only whiskey—scotch whiskey— could possibly fill it.

Until Ben. Ben was different because Ben was like the girls. Ben had an interior life. He read books, he went to films, and he wanted to discuss them. Ben anguished. He cried at sad endings. Ben was a fag and everyone, including Father Michael John, knew it, even though Ben at only fifteen probably hadn't fully realized it yet. Father Michael John, pastor of Holy Redeemer's, reflected upon it and concluded that fooling around with Ben simply would not count against his celibacy, because that kind of fooling around wasn't really sex anyway. He'd only be hanging around with a boy. Father Michael John O'Sullivan really wanted the girls. He considered that mere *attraction* to the opposite sex was the actual sin against his celibacy, of which near occasion he had to avoid at all costs. All the more reason to frequent Ben's company. Anyone could see Ben needed help and that Father Mike was just the one. Big, strong shoulders, full head of hair, Irish as the day was long, clearly a man's man just reaching out to help the poor homo kid.

"Wanna' go for some ice cream, Ben?"

> (Spot up on Ben and Michael John sitting next to each other in the front seat of an automobile; this is on the platform raised above the stage. They are eating ice cream cones. They stare straight ahead. They sit with feet flat on the floor and knees together. Perpetua, stage center, is alone.)

Perpetua knew, just knew, what was happening, even though she did not have the words for it. And did she ever breathe a sigh of relief about the fact that at least it wasn't going to involve another priest, and surely not a woman. No harm then. Not in the long run. Let him have his fun; he's a man after all. A man first and priest second.

Oh, for the nuns it was the opposite. Once a nun, the woman part died. Any girl for whom that was not true got drummed out early on. Early on. They'd send a letter to her parents, "Come and get her. Come and get her now."

Responsorial Psalm

[Depending upon liturgical reasons, response may be
"Everybody knew" or "Nobody knew."]

✳Linda Holt's father touched her breasts in the back seat of their family's station wagon.

Response: And everybody knew. [*See above*, or "Nobody knew."]

Janie O'Hare was gang-raped in the bushes by the baseball field.

Response: And everybody knew.

Tommy Hanrahan's mother fed him cornflakes for dinner every night. And didn't Father Michael say to send him down to the rectory any time, he'd look out for him?

Response: And everybody knew.

Mary Michaels was dating a black kid on the sly.

Response: And everybody knew.

Tommy Hanrahan's father was sleeping with Janie O'Hare's mother.

Response: And everybody knew.

Bobby Slattery was a twenty-four-hour-a-day drunk by the time he was fourteen.

Response: And everybody knew.

Patty Steven's uncle who lived with them had killed a pedestrian in a hit-and-run.

Response: And everybody knew.

He was a drunk … and everybody knew. He watched her, Patty, and maybe he touched her and maybe some wondered.

Response: And everybody knew.

Gospel

Burning coal[4]

(A priest, standing in a pulpit, makes a wriggling gesture with his thumb on his forehead, on his lips, then on his heart. At the foot of the pulpit is a circle of men and women seated in chairs, some holding babies. The women wear large hats and the men hold their hats on their laps. They stand and make similar wriggling gestures themselves, shush their children, and then tilt their heads up, craning them back to show attention to the priest in the pulpit, to the Gospel. In turn, the priest makes a wriggling gesture on the huge open book in front of him. He opens his hands then, in what appear to be parentheses over the book, and they hear his voice going in and out of range.)

*At about 5:30 every morning, except Sundays, Elmira gets the mail. She squeezes her two hundred pounds onto the bottom step of their front hall staircase, and then waits until the letter carrier squeaks open the mailbox lid at around 10:00. Once she hears his footsteps change

---

4. In the prayer the priest silently prays before proclaiming the Gospel, he begs in the words of the prophet to have his lips cleansed with burning coal. Picturing that, imagining that, could send a congregant reeling for minutes and minutes worth of missing the words of the Gospel.

from being on wood to cement, she lunges as fast as she can for the doorknob, because a thief follows the letter carrier.

Elmira grabs the stuff crammed into the little black metal box and presses all of it between her palms as if she were flattening a hamburger patty. Then she grunts her way up the stairs to the second floor where the kitchen is, slowly swinging her elbows wide, side to side, looking the way an elephant does when it walks. There's snorting involved, too, just like an elephant would do. She's wearing one of the johnnies from the state hospital, wrinkled and gray.

Up in the kitchen, Michelle Joanne—MJ, the patients call her—scrapes egg off the dishes. She startles at a man's voice in the adjacent room.

"Get your ass outta my face, you bitch!"

Harold's bumped into Elmira again, Michelle Joanne figures, as she scrapes egg off dishes in the kitchen sink. Michelle Joanne—MJ—hears the scuffle of their feet shuffling and Elmira's grunting. *She's probably butting him with her head.*

MJ leaves them alone as she hears him run down the stairs, mumbling, "Bitch. Goddamn bitch." MJ knows he's late for his job at Lightpost, where he puts game pieces into plastic bags. *Good thing they understand Harold over there,* she shakes her head, *good thing they know about once a month he'll call everybody in sight a goddamn fucking son-of-a-something.* MJ looks out the window over the sink. *When he says his "bad words," he fans his fingers over his mouth and rubs his chin real hard. The nuns must have washed out Harold's mouth with soap but good, once or twice.*

"Hey, Harold, have a nice day now," she yells after him. He slams the door so hard, she almost drops a dish. MJ loves him. Elmira too. All of them. Twenty-six over the last two-and-a-half years. They come and go. They're winos and ex-cons and psychos. They chew and they piss and they cry. And they laugh. Clearer and truer than any of the Junior Leaguers she ever ate quiche with. These people were prime colors-- bold and real and not pastel at all.

"Cut that liberal half-assed shit, Michelle Joanne. We're the poor of America," her then husband had yelled one day when he'd been leaving for the office, his gray three pieces immaculate, his tie, silk.

She was shocked; Leonard had finally yelled.

She'd figured that what he meant about their being poor was that their pharmaceuticals had closed lower, or, something. He'd wagged that day's Wall Street Journal under her nose and curled his lips with such revulsion, he looked as though he wanted to blast her out of this world. He also sprayed her with his spit, just a little. He tried to catch it with his teeth, but it dribbled onto his chin, instead, and he had to wipe it off.

He will never forgive me for that, MJ remembers thinking. In a way, she knew then he would have to divorce her because he had lost his spittle in her presence, a shame that could not be healed.

During the divorce, Leonard fought for things like the mink coat he had bought her for her thirty-fifth birthday, but which she'd long since sold, giving the money to Oxfam. He didn't understand any of it.

"Your Honor, if we'd had children—and I thank God we did not—I'd be fighting for full custody now to protect them from this Moonie cult that has robbed my wife of her senses—" he'd said.

"Not to mention the mink coat, right, Len?" MJ said.

"Your Honor, I object!"

"The husband can't object." The judge slammed her gavel. "You are not counsel in this case."

Apparently, Leonard had thought that MJ's leaving him for a "Christian community house devoted to serving destitute street people" somehow robbed him of his masculinity (whenever he said that phrase, "Christ-i-an," "commUNity," he made a shrugging gesture and crabbed two fingers of both hands in the air to mean both quote/unquote and disdain all in the one move).

"Another man, I could understand, forgive," Leonard had said. "Another woman, even ... but this—"

"Leonard, you are overreacting."

"Overreacting? My wife—"

"Ex-wife." MJ tossed that one pointedly.

"Soon to be ex-wife takes off for life on a funny farm in Roxbury, no less, investing good money—"

Family House had been her dream in college. Surely that was before MJ had ever met Leonard, back when she was Michelle Joanne O'Brien. Anne had died giving birth to Michelle—her ninth child—in 1956. MJ's friends, Jambo and Barbara, and she would talk for hours about selling everything they had and buying a three-decker that they'd fix up and turn into a community for street people. By the time Jambo had announced he'd found a house for them, it was ten years later and MJ was having discussions with Leonard about whether to furnish their patio with a six-hundred-dollar black mesh patio set, market umbrella and all. So it hadn't simply surprised Leonard when she'd asked for six thousand dollars for a down payment on Family House; it had jolted him right into the end game.

With the divorce settlement funds, MJ pitched in her six thousand, and Jambo and Barbara and she started the rehab. On their first visit to the property, the bushes ballooned out a foot over the tops of the first-floor windows. The second stair leading up to the front porch had collapsed. The porch itself tipped down into the house, so you slid into the front door. The large oval window on the front door was boarded with plywood and painted over in misspelled swear words and "Yanke go hom."

In the front hall, the stench was a combination of winos and dog urine imbedded in damp plaster. The wallpaper peeled at the edges in dark, browned curls, and it had a pattern that looked like perspiration stains. Jambo reached up and pulled on the overhead bulb. The effect of the sudden spotlight was gruesome. Things scurried as if hit with hot water. The bulb swayed wildly and the dust particles floated clearly in the light, so many and so thick, it was like snow. MJ gagged.

"Any mail?" MJ asks Elmira. MJ is up to her elbows in the a dishpan. They get a lot of mail. They are on every mailing list at Family House: Catholic Connection, Amnesty International, Christians for Community Living, all of the vegetarian and pacifist and nuclear lists, feminists lists, Clamshell, Network, Former (which was ex-priests), Vow (which was married ex-priests), Dignity (Catholic gays), and on and on.

It is MJ's day "in." They each take one day "in," and they all take Sundays to pray together as a community. "In" just means cleaning and cooking and mending and washing. Endless work. The kitchen grease alone would take a month of "ins" to dissolve. Jambo does a Thai fry every Friday, vegetables in hot sauce so spicy your eyebrows catch the sweat and you beg for mercy. He fires up his wok and throws some broccoli and cabbage into the oil, and it spatters all over the wall.

The mess gets to MJ a little, but it drives Barbara crazy. She was in the convent for a while where housecleaning had an escatalogical purpose. She'd finally given up on converting them to being immaculate, even clean. Now she just kept her own room the way she needed it to be. Not only clean, but pretty. The poster on her door, really a page out of an old

Newsweek, a Corita print, reads, "Every pebble in the ocean affects the ocean." Her curtains match her bedspread, and her books are in crates that are stacked sideways, so it looks like a library. She also has a prayer corner, complete with candles and a Bible and a cross made from Puerto Rican palm leaves, all set on a small rug that matches the curtains that match the bedspread.

MJ likes to slip into Barbara's room when the house is empty, which is rare, even though one of their agreements is that personal space is private. Barbara would never mind, but MJ doesn't tell her because the secrecy makes it seem even more like an escape. They have no locks on any doors, not even the front door, so sometimes MJ just goes into Barbara's room and the blue-green curtains and the blue-green bedspread and the blue-green rug ebb around her, and she floats for a minute or two. The lingering odor of incense touches her cheek like a ghost would, a kind ghost.

"Elmira, there's Ski!" MJ pulls a dishtowel down from its hook and mashes it in her hands to get them dry.

Two houses down, Ski's weaving through the shrubs that climb all over the porch railing of the gray house. He's the mail thief. Everyone in the neighborhood calls him Ski because of the hat, a red stocking cap that falls in a tapering trail down his back. The kids come up behind him and pull on it, sometimes, but they are afraid of him: he looks like he can work magic. He is toothless and some of his fingernails are almost two inches long. You can't tell what race he is or what nationality or even how old he is. His skin is so dirty and infested that it moves slightly, as if alive.

They have Ski arrested whenever he steals anything important—like last February when he grabbed Mrs. Vidal's disability check out of her mailbox just as she was getting to the front door. MJ and Barbara and Jambo worked it out that the cops call it vagrancy and Family House tries to curb his felonious activities. But every time they ask Ski to move into Family House, he says the same thing: "Say what? Stay with you white folks, living like poor folks? You crazy, man? This here's my crib, man," and he points to his leather pouch stolen from an unsuspecting postal employee. In it, he stashes everything he owns.

Ski's pulled himself up off the ground now and is leaning over the railing, his bottom—just bones—threatening to punch straight through his pants. Goodwill specials, they are, jersey knit women's pantsuit pants. Vintage. They're dark green and, with his red hat, he be the ghetto's Christmas elf.

"You get outta there, Ski!" MJ yells. Ski pushes off the railing backward and lands like a cat, strolling off with a rhythm in his hips that makes his satchel swing a little.

Coffee's done. It pours red-brown mahogany into her mug, her special mug that her lover Christine, former nun, had wanted to give her for their second anniversary last September. The mug reads, "Trust in God" where mugs usually have their messages, but then inside on the bottom it says, "*She*'ll provide."

They'd planned that, every year, they would take the wedding pictures and the written ceremony back to the Unitarian church on their anniversary and do it all over again, just for themselves. But last September, the night before what would have been their second anniversary, Christine was on her back in their bed—really just a mattress on the floor—staring off into the distance. MJ had the feeling, standing there and slipping out of her T-shirt, that she was watching her sweetheart float on water. She could hear just the edges of Jambo's voice talking to a new resident guest, Bobby Smith. Then she spoke.

"I saw that priest my sisters always talk about—that Father Michael John—today." MJ pulled on her nightgown. "At the grocery store. He was stealing cans of crabmeat. I couldn't believe it. I felt so bad for him."

"I love you, Mickey Jo."

"I love you, too, gentle lady." MJ had dropped to her knees on the mattress and nested herself onto Christine's soft, full chest. Christine's voice, when she wanted it to, could gather itself inside her chest and make a procession out to an audience. MJ whispered, "Hon, there must be a moment before an ordination, a month before, sometimes only a day, when the ordinands—"

Christine laughed softly, "Such a big word."

"When the ordinands," MJ continued, "surely must look at their hands, feel them, feel the way they have always felt real and as belonging to them." Tears now slid down the cracks of wrinkles at the corners of MJ's eyes onto Christine's breasts. "And they must then realize that these hands do NOT belong to them at all any more. They are God's and they are instruments that God will use. Sweetie, I want to add something to our ceremony tomorrow—"

Christine felt a twinge of envy that she was never as romantic or thoughtful—or so capable of innocent belief—as MJ could be. Their bodies shifted, but they stayed layered together. "I want to say—" MJ curled her legs behind Christine's, "that when we touch each other, God happens. We make Eucharist of each other, we consecrate each other."

They heard Jambo's screams, then, and Christine jumped up to see what was wrong.

> (Spot up on woman sitting, looking out a window, holding coffee mug, wearing an apron. She speaks, dreamlike, as if reciting poetry.)
>   WOMAN IN APRON:

What got me off thinking about this? Nipping month of May, black coffee, oh, my mug, maybe. Geranium plant adding its touch of life and beauty no matter how meager. Elmira happy, eating her bananas in her room with lots of crunchy stuff. And just me, quiet, and the mail. And maybe that bird will come back and sing.

> (Priest glances up and out at the assembled.)

>   PRIEST:

This is the word of the Gospel.

> (Those assembled bend to sit, showing more interest in adjusting their seats and quieting their children than in responding to the priest. They toss their antiphonal answer in a rote, memorized, mumbled way.)

>   ASSEMBLED:

Praise be the word of God.

The Homily

✳"First of all, we do not call it a sermon, we call it a homily." Sister Mary Perpetua looked out at her class of eight- and nine-year-olds who had never heard either of the words before. They looked up at her, some scratching their noses, some fumbling with buttons, some deeply staring at their inner screens which reflected games or cartoons.

"A *sermon* is what Protestants have at their Sunday services, which are not Masses and which do not fulfill any of the obligations." Perpetua walked back and forth in the aisle as they sat, trapped, in the pews of their catechism class. "*Their* sermons need not be about the text of the day, dear children. They are no more than speeches. While a homily is an explanation of the Gospel of the *day*, a teaching. It strays not from the word of God in the Bible. It offers no personal opinions on behavior or ethics, but rather it takes the parable presented and unlocks its mystery for us, for we could not understand the parable unless the priest from his training and in his wisdom and as a result of the grace of his ordination unveiled the parable for us. Oh, there is ego in the Protestant sermon, dear children. There is pride."

Perpetua closed her eyes as she spoke this and shook her head sadly but with a decidedly she'd-known-it-all-along look on her face.

"The Protestant minister might say to him*self*, 'I will speak on greed this week.' Then he shuts himself *away* in a study, a library, and writes his *own* essay, my dears, on greed. Our good priest, however, humbly presents himself before the word of God as proffered to him through the wisdom of the liturgical calendar and discovers that despite the goings-on of the current day, God, in whatever the day's Gospel is, presents a parable that will speak to us. That is the theme of his homily then: whatever is presented in the Gospel of the day, chosen for him by God and not by his own preferences."

In the first months after her arrival at Cathedral, she had put fear into them that screwed them to their seats, glued their arms to their sides. They behaved, because early on, the first week or so, they saw her toss Paul Connolly. Pick him up, one handed, and toss him. He had landed, skidding backward on his bum until he thwacked up against the front of the front pew. He got himself up and walked back to his seat, no problem. Said afterward in the yard that she hadn't hurt him at all. He'd been eight, though, and it must have hurt something in him, even if the bruises didn't show.

The children behaved for another reason: in a strange way, they rather liked Sister Mary Perpetua. Picking up and tossing one of them was clearly not a good thing, but she talked to them as though they were grown-ups. Even though they didn't understand her words, they felt she respected them in a way that their parents did not. Here they are in the church, which in itself is serious, and then they are talked to in an extraordinary, grown-up way. So they never, ever tell their parents about the Paul Connolly thing. Some of the parents were hitters anyway, of course, but even the hitters wouldn't want their kids tossed, well, carelessly thrown, really, as if discarded. So the kids never told.

As Perpetua talked on, some of the children paid attention to her shoes, the black leather worn thin, the shoelaces graying from years of twisting. Some of them watched her fingers fuss with her crucifix. The difference between a cross and a crucifix was another Protestant-versus-Catholic issue, Perpetua explained. The cross was just the sanitized, bare structure, symbolizing salvation and the Protestants' dislike of anything "liturgical" (meaning to them "lurid"). The crucifix was the cross with the body, the corpus, hanging on it, virtually naked, sagging in agony and humiliation. Some might say this difference showed that Catholics apprehended the flesh and blood of the incarnate Christ, revered the humanity in the divinity. Others might say it showed the punishment that would befall the sinner who indulged in the pleasures of the body. And some, let's say budding homosexual boys, might be imagining the organ hidden beneath the tiny spit of cloth draped around his hips, his loins, and attracted to the nakedness, to the edges the ribs made on his sides, to his offering his body. Those boys might bud, themselves, kneeling there. The thoughtful among them would never forget those stolen moments of fantasy and never forgive themselves for having such feelings for the Christ.

Perpetua's crucifix hung from a cord around her neck, which snaked under her gamp (the stiff shield that covered her chest from her neck to almost her waist.) The crucifix, about four or five inches long, was wedged under her leather cincture in the middle of her torso, the Christ's wretched arms and head peering over the three-inch wide belt, giving the effect of an effigy pinned to a clothesline. All the Mercies wedged their crucifixes this way so as not to bang them into desks. Once, playing dodgeball, one of the children shot the ball straight at Sister Mary Thaddeus, and it hit her so hard in the chest that it dimpled her gamp. The gamps back then were made of linen, starched to attention; that was before they switched to white plastic. The ball hit Thaddeus so hard that she flushed and giggled, straightening her rimless glasses, which had been jarred. Later, Margaret Griffin threw up cherries and the children all got to go home early.

The children named all the sisters "Stah" as they wildly waved their hands to be called on. "Call on me, Stah! Stah, call on me!" Sometimes, in fact often enough to begin to breed caution in them, their attention could be so deeply focused on being called to answer, that once having been called, the child would have no thing in her mind, no thing at all. Just panting and dryness from the hubbub of "Stah, Stah, me, Stah, me." The child would hear his name called and stand, and then a fraction of a minute later, the class would realize that "it" had happened to him (as it happened to somebody at least once a day), at which point the "Stah, Stah's" would erupt again, shaming the child into resuming his seat.

Sister Perpetua went on. "Our Lord could have spoken simply and clearly, but instead he spoke in parables so that our search for the truth would take us on a rich, complicated journey." Maureen Hennigan didn't that think that was right what Sister had just said. Maureen even thought, "No, wrong." Maureen knew the Gospel stories. They were like bedtime stories and nursery rhymes. They were pretty and they taught you something and you liked to listen to them because you could picture what was happening—like it was real and it was happening to you. It seemed to Maureen that the Gospel was full of good stories, not complicated journeys and searches. She went on and on, Sister Mary Perpetua, but since she wasn't telling stories none of the children listened to her very well.

There is a songbird that lives in the rafters of the cathedral, and either the janitor cannot reach it to shoo it away or he does not try to.

The bird is well-mannered and respectful of the liturgies, the incensing, the choir rehearsals, the bell ringing, and even the catechism classes. It chirps and swoops at Sunday Masses but never at Requiem Masses.

One Sunday, you could almost fear for the little thing, its joy so great it seemed more than its tiny body could handle. Before people arrived for Mass, Sister Mary Perpetua tried to "end this mockery of all that is holy" by chasing it, screaming, waving brooms and rags. It was she, of course, that made a mockery of all that is holy, and virtually everyone who witnessed her rage at the little songbird understood that perfectly. No one could remember Sister Mary Perpetua doing anything before the songbird incident that was so dramatic or that drew as much attention to herself. It was as if she had gone a little mad and there was no one to help her see it.

The community of sisters she lives with in the convent across the street are strangers to each other, purposefully so, that they might be more fully wedded to Jesus Christ and to his mission for them than to friendships. And besides, they have seen in her the pride of being a blood sister to a priest. They have seen it daily, preening itself like a cat licking its private parts, and they detest her for it.

Since his arrival at Cathedral, her brother has paid her no attention whatsoever. None. He carries it off that it would be unseemly to display their blood relation in any way. Aside from accompanying each other on All Souls' Day to the gravesides of their parents, they have spent no time alone in each other's company. But in reality, his withdrawal is not about unseemly displays or church politics or vows. It is not about anything more complicated that the fact that he has resented her proprietary interest in him his whole life, as he grasps that it is her way of living vicariously through him. She is the vulture and he the prey. He is here at Cathedral so he can be watched by the powerful powers that be, Perpetua's watchfulness merely an irritation. The hierarchy will wait until things seem settled, until he seems balanced, and then he will be sent to a single priest parish out near the orchards, where, if they discover he's doing it again, they will either make him a hospital chaplain or ship him to the southwest. Somehow, all of it feels like her fault. He detests her, simply put. Detests her.

After some months of Perpetua's presence at Cathedral, the children could tell she was not cared about. It might have been that a wisp of hair stuck out from underneath her wimple, wild and savage against the white of the starched linen, or that some food was lodged between her teeth and no one had told her. Perpetua's imperiousness was shrinking like a puddle in the sun, but as she became smaller and drier, she became meaner. Tossing Paul Connolly seemed the least of it, now. In front of the whole class, she told Maureen Hennigan that Maureen would die alone and drunk and in a gutter like Edgar Allen Poe because she, like the poet himself, was an only child in this church of propagation and in this land of plenty. Maureen would never know the love of a brother, Perpetua went on, and a greater love than this there is none. After class, Maureen Hennigan, who was nine, took the fifteen cents she had in her pocket and got on a city bus. She rode it around and around for hours until the police found her. Her mother, hysterical, had alerted them.

(A woman keens in a corner.)

"She's gone missing, my Maureen."And she being only nine years of age, being my only, only child …."

Then, there was the bat in the convent. She ranted, Perpetua did, and strode through the convent halls with her nightcap tightly tied onto her head, a broom firmly in her hand, hollering and hollering. The young nuns cowered in their rooms until finally the mother general stepped into the corridor where the bat was darting and Perpetua was flailing. Mother General Ambrose spat out one word: "Desist." That was just too much for Sister Mary Perpetua. She crumpled like a demon confronted with a silver cross.Then Ambrose instructed, "The chapel before morning prayer," and returned to her room, leaving Perpetua on her knees in the middle of the hallway. Perpetua leaned on the broom to get back to her feet and as she stood, the bat flew up behind her and swatted her on his way by. She jerked and let out a small, involuntary scream but found her way back to her room where she waited on her knees for dawn.

The parable Perpetua hated most was the lost sheep one. It made her frantic that the Good Shepherd would turn his back on the very ones that loved and obeyed him, leaving them vulnerable and alone and to their own devices just to find the one sheep stupid or wicked enough to get itself lost. It never seemed fair to the good ones. It never seemed fair. At some point in the future, if things were fair, Maureen Hennigan would be able to inform Sister Mary Perpetua, "You are missing the point of the parable of the lost sheep, Stah: all who hear it are themselves the lost sheep, *because all of us lose our way*. It is for you, Sister Mary Perpetua, that our Lord searches. It is you who is lost."

That would be a fair lesson to teach Sister Mary Perpetua about parables and homilies.

Creed

Credo

I believe

[All stand.]

✳During Holy Week, oil is blessed in the cathedrals of the world. Oil enough for the coming year, for every parish in every corner of every diocese. Oil for all of the baptisms to come, all of the ordinations—priestly and deaconate—all of the blessings of the sick and the annointings of the dead.

Huge Father Andrew Dolan, six foot four, at least, and three hundred pounds or more, bent over the tub of oil. The old tub's walls of thick, dull brass hinted at an industrial provenance, perhaps crafted by a laborer at some factory at the turn of the century. Some laborer, a comeover for sure, perhaps had stolen it, disabused his bosses of it, and for what? Perhaps the thief wondered, "What did the Yankees need this lurvely tub for? It was the priest who needed the tub for the annual oil and sure galvanized tin wouldn't do for the House of the Lord, wouldn't do at all."

Decades, generations later, Father Andrew Dolan picked up this old brass tub, this heavy half-barrel, and it *was* heavy, filled with all of the fine, pure oil for the sacraments of the year to come. He bent deep at the knees that holy day, his broad, huge back straight, his arms stretched around the tub in an embrace. Then he laced his fingers together and, with the aid of two little altar boys who guided the vat upward so it would not tilt or spill, he rose and steadied it, reachieving his equilibrium. Exertion was visible in the rippling clench of his jaw and in the red thickening of his neck inside the stiff white collar, which peeped out above the white alb, the dress-like garment that foamed around his frame.

Once upright and balanced, Father Andrew Dolan began to walk. Looking straight ahead, he thudded a slow solo procession down the center aisle to the back of the cathedral. The vat swayed very slightly, the lapping of the heavy oil against the thick brass was almost soundless under the more dense sound of his enormous feet striking the marble floor. He was abundance. His strength and his courage a colossus. He was God's guard and if he, the priest, were this tremendous, surely that meant God was great beyond imagining.

Bubbles of sweat surfaced, shining at the line of a solid black heft of hair. Sweat edged his upper lip, too. But his face was relaxed and his grip on the vat was hard and fast, not tense. There was no fear coming off of him, just pride and duty. People knew they could follow him into the desert and emerge unscathed. They knew they could be abundantly blessed and secured by following him who dared to serve the people so. In fact, it was all the congregation could do to keep from dancing, and in a way they did dance, in solemn, dignified measure behind this muscleman for Christ. He awed them, and they were blessed by their awe. Their attentiveness flowed out of them in reverent waves, out of them and onto the oil in the tub. Blessed be the babies baptized in that oil, and sure the sick will be saints, and the dead.

The giant used his strength to strengthen faith. His trip from the altar to the aisle's end was long and slow and riveting. Would he make it? Would the holy oil suffer a spill, would he slip? Would he cry out for help? Would he fall to his knees? Some in the congregation, the boys aged eleven and the men who had never succeeded at their chosen tasks, wished he would fall. However, the ones whose faith was only ever ratified, knew he would make it to the end of the aisle indeed before they knew he would even lift the tub. Others who watched and waited as he passed pew after pew, as he made it halfway and then more than halfway, felt their spirits begin to buzz and expand in their chests, felt their eyes open and their feet maneuver to spots inches off the ground. He would do it; he would do it!

And he did do it. He set the vessel down on a sturdy linen-covered table in the entryway, the vestibule. Any who had brought a vial or tiny bottle could have it filled with this holy oil, which had been blessed on this holy day by—whom shall we say? Shall we say Bishop Peter

Donoghue? Or this guardian giant, did he do the blessing? Or, was it his feat, his display of faith and pride and courage itself, was it that which did the blessing? Did the congregation's awe bless the oil, their awe at the giant's brand of humanness, at the fact that faith actually exists? Was it their belief in strength and abundance that blessed *it*, or did the oil bless *them* with that hope?

And his journey ... was it to Golgotha or was he Christopher?

Christ carried mortality; Mary carried eternity; Father Andrew Dolan carried, oh, he carried the very hope of the people.

> (Perpetua observes all of this, and, keeping it locked in her heart, ponders who would be named pastor of Cathedral: Andrew Dolan the Giant, or Michael John, her brother, who was not a giant at all?)

Offertory

Suscipe

ACT III: Accept

SCENE I: Procession
(Three women march in procession, one behind the other, down the middle aisle of a church. They are old, gray-haired, and rather worn, the skin on their bodies not taut, their cheeks wrinkled. One is very much older than the other two, but she moves with the fluid grace and dignity as the others. They walk—no, dance, really—very, very, slowly down the aisle. The first one has a long white linen cloth draped over her arms which are spread like a cross. She appears to be replicating what is called the resurrection cross, where the cloths that wrapped the body in the tomb, then useless, are draped over the empty cross to show the triumph over death. She turns slowly to the woman behind her, who reaches and out and takes the cloth from the first woman onto her own arms and then spreads her arms wide, again in the symbol of the resurrection cross. This second woman, thusly clothed, solemnly takes two steps and then turns to the woman behind her. The third woman repeats the action of receiving the drape and presenting herself as the resurrection cross to the assembled congregation. The three then circle the altar until the one with the cloth stands behind the altar with the other two on either side of her. The middle woman

then bows while the other two slowly remove the cloth from her shoulders, raise it, allow it to billow just slightly on the air before they lower it to the altar. All three women smooth the cloth with their palms. They bow in unison, then, leave the altar as they came, marching in procession down the middle aisle, slowly, their arms by their sides.)

SCENE II: Altar

✳Her body simply produces them. Extras of them. Platelets. A man in a coffee shop says to the counterman that he is an only child. Some kind of joke. She debates whether to admit she is one too—a singleton. And he then tells the counterman his theory—how people think only children are spoiled and cannot share, when the opposite is true. Only children, he says, act with generosity because they have never feared not getting their due. She could have confirmed his theory for him, told him she was just coming from donating platelets, a double dose in fact, nine cycles. Almost two hours of stillness and discomfort to give back what she produces in amplitude.

She could have told him by way of confirmation of his theory that she has never worried about money. She has always known there would be enough. The universe, by simply being, simply gives and gives and gives.

She knew two beggars when she was a child. One did not actually beg, but dressed and acted and moved through the world like a beggar. She walked all bundled up in a brown wool overcoat, whatever the weather, and always wore a knitted hat pulled tightly down on her head like a sock over a darning egg. Jennie was her name. She was never violent, far from it, although her appearance scared the children. None of the kids had heard her even speak. She walked in the gutter of Pleasant Street, walked its two-and-a-half-mile length into downtown and then its two-and-a-half-mile length back to where she lived in a room. And she did this as many times a day as could fit into daylight. She scuffled her feet—someone was obviously paying to keep her in shoes, or else she was an heiress, a possibility. She walked with her shoulders stooped and she looked at nothing but her feet and the gutter. She sensed traffic in order to avoid it, rather than looking up to see it coming.

On the rare occasion when the children saw her face, the long gray hairs that poked out in stiffened wisps from around her lips and inside her nostrils shocked them. Except for that her eyes looked runny and weak like a rabbit's, she could have been taken for a witch. She wasn't a beggar or a witch. She wasn't a wanderer either, since she never diverted from her Pleasant Street path. She was a commuter. Sunday through Saturday, rain, snow, or heat.

The beggar she knew who really begged, sat. He sat on a pad of blankets in the same spot when it was sunny and in a different spot when it was rainy. She'd see him on school days because her trek to get the bus for home passed directly in front of his station. He had no legs. He was always dressed exactly the same, in clothes fashioned together out of tightly woven wool blankets. Even the hat on his head, like a skullcap, was made from this material. It was tight like boiled wool, boiled in greasy water. Was he blind too? Her memory provides film-covered bluey sockets that bobbled uncontrollably, not following sound or light. But she is not confident that this is not only her imagination.

If anyone put a coin in the can he held up, that person was entitled to reach down right close to him into the other can where he kept the pencils and take one. But she had never seen even one person do that. Kids knocked the can over sometimes, sometimes on purpose, scattering the pencils, but he never flickered. He would feel for the pencils and set them right. He had crutches, stubs of crutches that swung his stubs of legs—but she'd never seen him use them. He was always sitting in place whenever she passed him, the crutches leaning against the wall next to him, ready to grab. That he ate or slept, sat on chairs or toilets was unimaginable to her, but she could imagine his swinging down the sidewalk suspended from the squat crutches. She could see the swagger he would have to conjure, creating forward propulsion by lurching side to side. He'd be like an engine of all kinds of motions, of all attitudes and trajectories.

He had a few teeth, which somehow was worse than having none at all. They were brown with cavities, like eyes on a potato. That was 1959 in Worcester, Massachusetts, Main Street, yet he looked like a picture from *Life* magazine from some country like Niger. His skin was dark, like the skin of a man on a camel—although under the blankets and the dirt and the years of sun exposure, his name could have been Danny Herlihy.

He was her model of a leper. It was clear that Jesus meant this particular beggarman in the greasy army-blanket clothes when he preached to her to love the poor. Other kids made fun of him and called him names that he was probably able to hear. She never did that. She always tried to have at least one coin to put into his cup every day. And she was not just keenly aware that she hoped the other kids could see her and realize she was better than they were. She was also supremely aware that Jesus was watching and that she was coming off very, very well.

(To allow you to give platelets, they ask you questions you must answer. Ever since 1977. Have you had sex with anyone from Niger? Or had sex with anyone who has, or shared a needle with anyone who had sex with anyone who has?)

Where did his legs go? He couldn't be a Vet, because they take care of their own. Jennie used her legs for just walking back and forth with no sense to her journey. What would he have done with legs?

The man in the coffee shop said, "Oh, it's always me, me, me," laughing because he'd assumed the sack of sandwich the counter guy had handed over was his order and not hers. That's what had gotten him started on the only child thing. Only child, male, he'd said, you know, always me, me, me. Only child, female, she'd said then, even though she never spoke to strangers.

She had spoken. Didn't that demonstrate the generosity and thoughtfulness of only children—prove, well, at least indicate that only children were not spoiled (such a rancid, horrible word)? Isn't the point that she'd connected with him, however briefly, in a wonderfully urban way, philosophers of the coffee counter, those two? They had smiled, accepted something from each other. In the movies—even on prime-time television—the next scene would be blouse unbuttonings and frantic tumblings, rough groans.

She took the brown bag and headed for the Public Garden to sit and eat her lunch.

The Collection

ACT IV: Ding a ling

SCENE I: Typewriter Keys

(Spot on Smoking Woman sitting in front of a typewriter on a small wooden desk downstage center. Facing the congregation, she types in a rhythm while she speaks, her words punctuated with the dinging bell of the return carriage. Behind Smoking Woman, two men in suits walk side by side toward her, each holding a green-felt lined basket connected to a six-foot-long handle, the total construction looking like a giant tablespoon. The men stop, genuflect as if to her back, turn their backs to each other and stretch, and then pass the baskets back and forth along each of the pews. There is no sound of change clinking because the basket is lined with heavy green felt.)

SMOKING WOMAN:

✴Dear Bishop Bythabuk, which is actually your name I am not making that up, well, actually I am, you are Bishop Peter Donoghue but because you follow the rules with no exception (except when it involves a transfer to the southwest), I call you Bishop "By the Book." Bishop Bythabuk.

I completely agree with you, which may seem to be a very strange thing for me to say, given several of my propensities so to speak. [Ding-ding-ling]

I felt I had to write. [Ding-ding-ling]

Congratulations on the letter you sent to your priests forbidding them to let groups use any Catholic facilities for their meetings if women's ordination is to be discussed. I think that it is about time that you be the Catholic in the equation, because then those who are fighting for changes in the Catholic church like women's ordination can clearly line up on the other side of the equation. [Ding-ding-ling]

As I see it, as long as the "Catholic" in the equation is wishy-washy and allows the "enemy" to hold meetings on Catholic hallowed/owned ground, well, it confuses things. It allows revolutionaries to deceive themselves into thinking they can still be, still are, Roman Catholic.

> (Smoking Woman stands, slowly walks around her typing table, takes the time to light a cigarette, drag on it strongly, pace, as if thinking of her next words. She has an "aha" moment and quickly sits and begins typing again.)

Dear revolutionaries who call yourselves Feministachurch (Could I make that up?) [Ding-ding-ling]:

Since you are pro-choice [Ding-ding-ling], pro-contraception [Ding-ding-ling], pro-divorce and -remarriage [Ding-ding-ling], pro-women's ordination [Ding-ding-ling], pro-same-sex unions [Ding-ding-ling], pro-using-the-word-Goddess-to–refer-to-the-divinity [Ding-ding-ling] [Ding-ding-ling][Ding-ding-ling], why again, would you want to hold your meetings on property owned by the Roman Catholic church?

I have heard many members of Feministachurch say that they cannot, will not, be driven out of "their" church, that they are Catholic and ... that it is the pope who is not.

I even know what they mean. They mean a church of love and equality is their church, a church based on Jesus' teachings; not this church that has been corrupted and is no longer the church that Jesus would recognize as his own, with its creed that has no mention of justice or love! They mean that their dreams of women priests and the equitable distribution of wealth are the true Catholic church. They think they have chosen the higher road, the harder road: to stay within the church and fight for change. Others who have left the church in droves, joined other denominations, started their own churches, or left organized religion entirely are seen by both orthodox Catholics and Feministachurchers to have sold out. The Feministas would add, they have taken the easier route by giving up on the patriarchal system instead of fighting for its change. But, listen, [Ding-ding-ling] I do not think I could find one member of Feministachurch who could say she believes in the concept, say, of "original sin" to any significant degree that would be recognizable as dogmatic by the Catholic church. [Ding-ding-ling] And if that is so, then we are not talking politics here alone. [Ding-ding-ling] This is not only about ordination for women or the right for women to choose contraceptives, let alone abortions, [Ding-ding-ling] or about free speech in the Catholic church (only Americans wonder why that isn't a right), or the end of mandated celibacy. This gets down to dogma.

For instance, who among you, Feministachurch, believes in the Virgin Birth? [Ding-ding-ling] The Immaculate Conception? [Ding-ding-ling] The Ascension? [Ding-ding-ling] The infallibility of the pope? [Ding-ding-ling] The kingship of Christ? [Ding-ding-ling] Transubstantiation? [Ding-ding-ling] The power of the priest to forgive sins?

Who among you, Feministachurch, believes these things in a way at all accepted by the Catholic church rather than nuanced and massaged and intellectualized beyond recognition? If even rank-and-file members of the Catholic church answered those questions truthfully, the numbers of congregants in the pews would shrivel. You would even lose a few priests.

(Smoking Woman stands and, holding a clipboard in her hands and wearing a whistle on a necklace of gimp around her neck, assumes the pose of an athletic coach.)

SMOKING WOMAN:

All those who believe in original sin as specifically laid out by the Catholic church, get in line here, please, behind Bishop Bythabuk. Those who have trouble believing in a system that factors in automatic sinfulness as the passkey to being human, okay, you line up too but way over there, on the other side of the fence.

You see, Mormons get to be Mormons (rather, members of the Church of Latter Day Saints—they should get to call themselves what they want to be called, too.) Roman Catholics get to be Roman Catholics and you don't, unless you believe their rules.

So, Bishop Bythabuk,

(Smoking Woman sits and begins typing.)

SMOKING WOMAN:

I agree with you. For years and years, I have stood outside the cathedral on ordination day alongside my Feministachurch friends and held a sign that simply read, "Ordain Women." I won't be doing that anymore because I understand now that you get to believe what you get to believe.

> (Smoking Woman stands.She half sits on the corner of the typewriter table and looks straight out at the assembly. She speaks in a conspiratorial tone.)

SMOKING WOMAN:
I'm collecting stories. There are thousands of them like this one.
Once upon a time there was a woman, a nun—Juliette we'll call her—and she had been a nun for over fifty years. She was not your television-stock-character nun; she was more like a Mother Teresa-type nun. She created a shelter for the sick and the homeless, the ones folks treated like lepers. And she raised money year after year to furnish the home with comfortable, lovely things, even providing roses for bedside tables. She played music for the people she called guests and they sang along. She lived in a rectory where an order of priests lived, and she had lived there for twenty years. She had seen their pastors come and go. She was on the staff of the church they served, so, when she wasn't ministering to the ones folks treated like lepers, she was ministering to the members of the parish. One day she was asked to serve at the baptism of a baby who had been adopted by two lesbian members of the parish, partners for fifteen years. Juliette wore an alb—a long white "dress" worn by altar servers and priests.

> (Spot up on Juliette standing on platform above the stage, wearing the alb. Frail, Juliette looks pale inside the alb, faint as if pigmented in strokes of pastel chalks by a shaking hand. Her appearance is in stark comparison to the youthful priest standing next to her in his vestments, deeply colored in rich , rich green.)

SMOKING WOMAN:

The couple had requested that Juliette join in the ceremony. The priest had suggested she don the alb. On her own she picked up the stole, the ribbon-like sash that hangs around a priest's neck when he administers sacraments. She chose a stole in rainbow colors, because the rainbow is a symbol of the gay community and because, out of vanity but not egregiously so, she wished to add color to her appearance, which she knew looked pale and gray and elderly. It was vanity, then, that led her to the stole; such a simple vice. It was not the vanity of presuming herself to be an ordained priest when in fact she was just a vowed religious sister with fifty years of experience. She was just helping, and truth be told, she wanted to look pretty for this occasion, which was so happy and important for this couple, her friends.

And so, she was fired.

It is said a canon lawyer-priest reported her to Bishop Bythabuk for assuming priestly duties in administering a sacrament. In the absence of a priest, in an emergency, on an ice floe, say, in the Arctic Circle, or in an emergency room with a dying infant, a lay person can administer baptism, and canonically nuns are considered mere lay persons. In this particular situation, however, standing as she was next to an ordained priest with no emergency apparent, no ice, no floe, no shortage of priests, Juliette had broken canon law when she picked up the little jar of holy oil, that oil blessed during Holy Week for all the annointings of the year to come. When she picked up that little jar of holy oil and blessed the baby with the words of the sacrament of baptism, Juliette had sinned.

After twenty years in the same living quarters, with the same alley view, the same single mattress and worn-out rug, her seventy-two-year-old self was ordered out. She was given no grace period, not even time to say good-bye to her parish with dignity. She was just fired. Without a pension, of course. With no place to live (nuns don't automatically have convents with extra beds waiting for them).

Juliette could think back on that moment when she had put the priestly stole around her neck. and she could accept fully and thoroughly and deeply her sin of vanity, wanting to plump up the color around her face. Too, Juliette could remember picking up the little jar of holy oil called chrism, the oil used at baptisms and ordinations, she could think back on that moment when she smoothed her fingertips with the holy balm and touched the infant's dusky skin. How I love you, she had thought at that moment and had felt as if God were speaking those words through her to this child, through her very fingertips. How I love you.

The argument ran: She knew the rules. The bishop had the right to kick her out.

Did I mention this is the same bishop who, for decades, transferred pedophile priests from parish to parish and to the Southwest?

Could that please be repeated?

Did I mention this is the same bishop who, for decades, transferred pedophile priests from parish to parish and to the Southwest?

In boldface, please?

Did I mention this is the same bishop who,for decades, transferred pedophile priests from parish to parish and to the southwest?

Shame on Juliette for hanging a priestly stole around her neck and thinking I love you, how I love you. Shame.

The moral of this story is this, Feministachurch: Get out of Catholic church halls and convent recreation rooms and Catholic college auditoriums and high school gyms. Stop baptizing your children in that church. Stop being married and buried in that church. Stop being employed by that church. Stop donating and attending, and stop insisting you are the Catholic in the equation. You are not. Build your own church. [Ding-ding-ling] Ordain your own priests. [Ding-ding-ling] Minister to your people. [Ding-ding-ling] BE the church of Jesus you search for. [Ding-ding-ling]

> (Smoking Woman rips the piece of paper out of the typewriter with a flourish and gives it a victory wave over her head. She tosses it into the collection basket that one of the men proffers to her, and then she walks downstage and exits.)

Lavabo

(The washing of the hands)

✳Up behind the house they held hands, Georgie and Molly. He was the one, he was, to see her first. He swore, from the moment he saw her red-gold hair turned about in the thick braid, he knew he loved her. His body moved whenever he caught a glimpse of her.

His thumb rubbed little circles over her palm. They looked out over the field to the hills. They hardly ever said a word. They would meet there at sunset, when her "Da" would be milking, his father would be adding up the till, and mothers would be lost in the chaos of supper. So, no one would notice.

He was thirty-two, then, and his family had resettled in Cowskeep from Belfast, some said, because his father had owed a great deal of money. His father took over the pub in Cowskeep, but he was the scallywag-type, full of stories and laughter, so the Catholics let themselves forget he was an Orangeman from the north. His humor felt so much like theirs, it was hard to believe he wasn't one of *them*.

"He's a good man, he is," one neighbor would say to another on the swaying walk home after "Hurry up, please, it's time."

"And you know I wouldn't be saying that with Danny me brother dead at their hands and all, excepting that he just don't seem like them others."

They'd nod in agreement, and gradually all the regulars were back at the pub even though an Orangeman was running it now. Georgie's job was to clean up the place. Took pride in his glasses' gleam, in the brilliance of his brass footrail.

He'd seen her across from the pub, a basket over her arm—maybe holding eggs—and that hair, red-gold in a woven flow down her back. *There she is,* he thought. *There she is.*

He'd known his approaching her was another thing entirely. Men did not speak to women whom they did not know until there was a proper introduction. Yet no one would introduce, properly or not, an Orangeman's son to a girl who was Catholic let alone only half his age. Even Georgie knew the story of Romeo and Juliet from the puppet shows that had come through when he was a child, and he supposed the part he was attempting to play had no good end. But oh, that hair.

He never knew that it was really she who had seen him first. His apron was tied breast-high and stiffly covered him down to his ankles as he'd pulled out the trash to the alley behind the pub. Not quite a romantic first glance, given the trash and all, but he had a cut to his jib that spoke of pride and responsibility. She'd heard they were Protestants, this new family, but he didn't look it. He looked regular, like the other men—late to marry, as all not-first-born men were in this country, but many years older than she.

"We can't, is all. We can't." Molly had no tears left. Marrying was not possible. She had whispered the question in the confessional and the answer had been absolute.

"If I canna' have you, I'll have no one." Georgie raised his voice and whacked his palm against the earth between them, their picnic now over and done.

It wasn't his fault, many would say perhaps, a rage so full and so old would have had to erupt out of him at some point. You couldn't be Irish and not have the rage that was like an incurable congenital disease. North or Republic, it did not matter atall. The rage was there.

"I feel the same way, you know that, Georgie, with God as my judge. I'll stay a virgin because of you for as long as I live."

Something split inside of him. He, for sure, was not seeing her, his Molly, in front of him. He was seeing the whole of it, the hundreds of years of it: grand landowners from England and all the rest of Ireland eating dirt. *So what if I don't call on your pope for my answers? So what if my church-going is spotty at best? I'm baptized a Christian and as poor and low-down as any of you Catholics. Should be good enough for any of ye but 'tis not, not atall.*

He grabbed her by the shoulders—and she wasn't small, she had the strength of the farm girl she was—but the way he pinned her, there was not anything she could do. It was brutal, a bolt of lightening so fast, so hot, so powerful. Burning, it branded her insides forever. And then it was over and done. She'd fainted, lost her wits for a bit of a time, and when she opened her eyes, he was gone.

Getting back into the house was hard to do without Mum or Da seeing her, all scratched and dirty as she was, bleary-eyed from all the crying. Molly couldn't remember how she'd walked home, though she had the picnic basket with her so she must have wrapped the things and packed it all up. And two months or so later, when Mum knew Molly's bleeding had not come and that Molly was getting sick in the mornings, she took her husband aside: "It was that Protestant liquor-monger, I know it."

Molly was lucky, indeed. Her eye was purple and her eyebrow split, and all of it was swollen. At least one tooth was missing. Da had hit her hard. But when it came to it, he didn't push her to the floor or anything else that would have done harm to the baby. And when he had thrown her out of the house, he'd thrown money after her too.

She got herself a ticket and, at fifteen years and pregnant, she headed to America. There was nowhere else to go.

Outside of Boston, there was an orphanage run by nuns that had a maternity wing. The ones they took in, usually in their sixth showing month, were most often young girls "in trouble."

"I need your help, Sister," Molly said at the front door, fat as a cow.

The portress led her in. It was a given that the baby would remain with the sisters, otherwise why would the girls have come to them? So Molly's baby twins, an infant boy she never saw or held but was allowed to give a saint's name, Peter, screamed and kicked his way to life, to citizenship in America, and to separation from the sister he would never know, named Delia by the nuns.

They gave Molly three days' rest and it was wonderful. Clean sheets and all. The food was meager but hot. The nuns encouraged visits to the chapel, and Molly would shuffle down there to the Virgin's statue and rub and rub each bead against her thumb. No one atall promised that any of this life would make any sense. At least on *Mary's* flight to Egypt *she*'d had her husband, *she*'d kept her baby. Molly sighed, and the little candles in the wrought-iron stand in front of the statue rippled their flames in answer to her.

Taking the stairs to leave was not easy. Each step, her privates burned and ached and pained her. *Good luck to you now, Peter,* she tossed the thought back over her shoulder to him, as well as an afterthought to the little girl: *The nuns will name ye just fine and will be good to ye. Do your best.*

Molly would start a job as a live-in with a well-off Catholic couple that had one child, a daughter, Anne. That was tomorrow. Tonight she would spend in the back pew in the nearest church. No one would notice or care.

Raising Annie kept Molly alive. Annie's mother, frail and sickly, remained in the solarium in their house opposite the city's most lovely pond, all day, every day. Molly was certain Annie's mother did not even watch them as they made their way to the pond and around its rambling walkway; she would barely raise her head from her pillows. Having taken a look at Molly the first day of her employ, the mother had judged her responsible and so had abrogated her motherly duties immediately and completely to the live-in who talked very little and smiled rarely.

After months on the job, Molly appeared at the solarium archway, Annie in hand as she had done each day of her employ. Annie was dressed up for her walk, woolen leggings with matching overcoat, brown with brown velvet trim.

"We are going for our daily constitutional, ma'am." Molly turned to fuss with Annie's hat. "We'll be on our way now."

No answer from the pillows and satin coverlet, only a languid wave of the hand, a brushing away.

"That's that, then, Annie dear, say good-bye to your mother."

Annie and Molly left through the big front door that opened onto the wide porch, threaded and veiled with bare wisteria vines. "Off we go, then."

Molly never picked up Annie to make her way any easier. She was old enough, indeed, at twenty-four months, to take the steps on her own, and no matter how slow that made the going, the independence it was teaching was worth the pace.

"What shall we look for this January morning, Annie dear?" Some days it would be a hunt for flat little stones, some days for pinecones. In the spring they would listen for birds, Molly thought, although these city birds were nothing compared to the farm. Which she didn't miss for a moment. Not a moment. Molly squared her shoulders and crossed the wide Pond Street with her charge. This land by the pond was considered country and lower-class by the Boston gentry, the Beacon Hill kind, Yankees all. Newly minted Catholic businessmen were taking up residence there. Annie's Da—not that *they* would ever use that country bumpkin word—built churches. He was the only Catholic in the whole archdiocese with the expertise to do so. So instead of being

Catholic making you poor, as usual, John T. Cooney's being Catholic had made him rich.

Molly had heard he had been a lucky man his entire life, except for his choice of wife.

But they managed to keep that part quiet. Although the bishop knew and probably the local pastor, hardly any gossip escaped about the real cause of Mrs. John T. Cooney's sudden and unexpected demise, so the clerics found a way to allow a Catholic funeral anyway. . It was a mortal sin to commit suicide and it was clearly mandated that no suicide could be buried in the sanctified ground of a Catholic cemetery. And only Catholics were allowed to be buried in Catholic cemeteries. There was, of course, a monetary consideration to be factored in. A plot was valuable real estate. In fact, many of the poorest put themselves into hock to be able to vouchsafe their future burial in hallowed Catholic ground.

One day, still cold but the pond not still frozen, Mrs. John T. Cooney arose from her solarium couch and left the house, dressed only in her silk dressing robe imported from the Orient, peacock blue with black trim. No one saw her go, or at least no one reported so afterwards. It is probable she did not pause or reconsider, but rather, that she headed straight for the pond. Molly and Annie, on their daily walk, were probably on the exact opposite side from where Annie's mother entered the water. The pond was a half-mile across at least, so they neither saw nor heard when she slid herself, without tremor, without reaction, under the cold brown surface. Perhaps she had picked up two heavy rocks and held them or filled the pockets of her robe with them to force her sinking. Molly and Annie, no doubt, had walked right by the spot on their way back to the house.

And so Molly's standing as Annie's surrogate mother became an established reality. Annie's father, mostly absent anyway, drowned his sorrow, as they say, in work, accepting jobs in the new diocese of Worcester. It was as a result of one of those positions that he moved them—Molly and Annie, the driver and the cook—to Worcester to live. A new diocese was burgeoning there. There were dozens of churches to be built and John T. Cooney was the man.

You lived in the Catholic section of the city. Whether your house was grand or whether it was a flat in a three-decker, you all lived within blocks of one another. You grew up in each other's families, rushed in through your neighbor's screen door without a knock, played catch in another backyard without asking whether Robbie, who lived there, was home or not. Every house had a minimum of three children, most a half a dozen or more. Three children, however, stood outside this close-knit neighborhood circle. They stood together alone. Michael John, his sister Josephine, and the new girl, Anne.

Anne looked up to the other two more than to anyone else. They were a little older, and Anne always wanted to play with the big kids. She especially wanted to play with them because they seemed so serious and grown-up. They would play school, she thought, not war always. And they shared a common reality: their mothers were both dead.

That fact partly accounted for the separateness between them and the neighborhood kids, but the distance was also because of schooling. Michael and Josephine went to the nuns on scholarship, but most of the neighborhood of Main South couldn't afford the twenty-five-dollar annual tuition so they went to the public down the block, Merrymount Elementary. Anne's father had a lot of money from building churches and from, some would later say, dealing in the liquor business, but her father had given up on the Church with a capital C. He built them, but he wouldn't go to them. So, Anne went to public.

At Children's Mass on Sundays, the parochial schools kids sat together up front while the Merrymount kids had to sit together in the back pews. After all, the Merrymount kids might have snot on their shirtsleeves or something else dirty, and the kids from Our Lady of the Angels would be scrubbed raw. Also, the OLA crew knew exactly when to stand, to kneel, to sit, to stand again. They were up front to lead the way, like the undertakers who always sat up front at requiems so the fallen-away wouldn't embarrass their relatives by not remembering when to kneel and stand.

Anne was girls regular. Straight-across bangs, Peter Pan collars. Michael and Josephine's parents were comeovers and so was Anne's nanny, but Molly made sure Anne was an all-American. Josephine was always in a skirt one size more than her age, regardless of her actual size: at six, she wore an eight; at eight, she wore a ten,. Her mother, believing in modesty at all costs, had insisted her daughters' clothes were to hang in toga-like folds, hiding her body's natural outline. Michael John was forced to wear his hair in shoulder-length ringlets until he was in third grade because a man's style of haircut was allowed only when long trousers replaced the child's short. And that substitution didn't happen back in Ireland until eighth grade, so third grade for Michael was quite a concession and was only due to his mother's familiarization with American ways. Not one of the American boys had hair like his beyond their fourth birthdays. That kind would taunt him when he passed with, "Girlie, girlie!" Boys from the Catholic neighborhood Main South, on the other hand, appreciated his humiliation and silently thanked God their mothers were modernizing at a quicker pace than Michael John's.

They played baseball in the street. There weren't many cars and there was no such thing as speeding, so the street was a safe enough ball field. They could not slide, however. A fall reminded them keenly that their neighborhood did not have a nice green park where landings would be softer, bruises not bloody, scrapes and cuts not the result. Anne liked dodgeball better, unless the boys started aiming the ball, flinging it like a stone in a slingshot, determined to actually hurt the one in the middle. She'd started her curse earlier than anybody else, so she opted out of any running games for one week of the month, and in the summer, no swimming that week either. She found during those weeks that she would seek out Josephine, and often Michael would join them and they would sit on the porch of Michael and Jo's three-decker and read. Sometimes Anne would have a magazine and they would pass that around.

Life. Huge photographs from all over the world. Pictures of automobiles and beautiful women. Bad times in Oklahoma, beautiful skies in Montana. They learned America reading *Life*. The three hardly talked at all. It seemed that Jo suffered Anne's company in silence, and for sure she rarely if ever left Anne and Michael alone. She had proprietorship, Jo did, and she never let Anne forget it.

It was extremely hot that day. The air was so dead and still and heavy you felt you were being kept in place.

Michael John said, "Anne, I think I would like to draw a picture of you. Would you mind?"

Jo gasped as it she'd been struck from behind, but said nothing.

"I would like that very much, Michael, thank you. What would like me to do?"

Anne was already smoothing her Peter Pan down flat and feeling, well, like she was going to be in *Life* magazine. Michael pulled out, from a spot under his wicker chair, a sketchpad and some pencils that were different from ordinary pencils.

"You sit over there," he motioned. Anne moved her chair to the corner of the piazza near the flower and he nodded, "Perfect."

Jo moved her place, too, right next to her brother, and watched while a picture that really looked like Anne unfolded. "Where did you ever get these pencils and this fancy paper?" she asked him accusingly as if it were some suspicious activity or else she would have known about it.

Michael smiled. "I'll do you next, sister dear."

"And how did you learn to do this?"

"The five'n'ten is where I found my supplies, and, I don't know how I learned to do this … I just did."

It was very hot and Anne knew she was not supposed to move a muscle, so she did not. She could feel sweat drooling down her spine and into the crack in her fanny. *Ooh, hot.* The privilege, however, of not only being accepted onto their porch but also being invited to be the subject of a portrait implied almost too much status for Anne to bear. She would not move. She would be perfectly still for as long as necessary.

Michael John and Jo's mother had died when Jo was just thirteen, their father already dead. Jo took up raising them both, which wasn't too unusual at the time. There was money enough from what Mother left to keep them in their three-decker flat and money enough for food. The nuns gave them each a scholarship, so tuition was not a worry. They kept on, really, without much difference to their lives at all. When Michael John graduated from high school, Jo was already a legal secretary at a firm downtown. A crackerjack she was, everyone said so. That she could have been a lawyer occurred to no one, least of all to herself.

Michael John announced over the kitchen table the night after his graduation, "Jo, it's the priesthood for me."

She looked over at him, pushed the salt and pepper his way, and pondered his very serious face. "You have felt the call?"

He nodded, tucking a forkful of pot roast and mashed potatoes into his mouth. She wanted so to ask him what that call was actually like. The nuns never described it; they just prayed you would get it. She held back from asking, as it seemed too intimate a question, something left for just him and God.

"Do you have a plan then?"

The Bible story of—is it Samuel?—who is asleep and hears something that wakes him up. "Who is there?" he cries to no answer, so he falls asleep again. Once more he hears something, his name—he *is* being called. "Who is there?" he cries and this time he is answered. It is the Lord. Samuel yells, "Here I am!" but then follows that declaration with a summary of what he thinks about the probability that, indeed, the Lord would be calling *him*: "Is it *I*, Lord?" In other words, "Are you sure, Lord, you really want *me*?"

For Michael John it didn't happen that way. Michael John had what was called a devotion to the Blessed Sacrament. The consecrated host, now the body of Jesus Christ, second person of the triune God, rested in a little golden box, the tabernacle, in the middle of the altar. If a person could accept that, why would he or she ever move from the pew in front of that miracle? Michael, often, only wanted to be there, kneeling in front of the tabernacle, knowing God was there ... *there*. Every first Friday of the month, Mass was followed by the rite of Holy Benediction. The host, a large one, was placed inside a small glass window in the center of a huge gold cross. The four corners of the cross, created by the intersection of the vertical piece with the horizontal one, were elaborately filled with great golden rays, as if from a sculpture of the sun. This artifact was called a monstrance, meaning it was designed to show, to demonstrate, the host of the body of Christ.

There was nothing better than Holy Benediction, Michael thought. The hymn was "Tantum Ergo," and it amazed him how everyone in the church knew the Latin words of all the verses. After the end of the Mass, as usual, the priest disappeared at first, but people stayed knowing what was to come next. Out the priest would come from the sacristy, enveloped in a floor-length cape, a cope it was called, made out of truly gold fabric, very heavy and rich. Over the cope was a special wide stole that the priest used to cover his hands when he picked up and carried the monstrance. And high he would lift it, the altar boys processing ahead of him swinging their thurifers of incense, the people sinking to both knees venerating the Blessed Sacrament just as the monstrance passed them and then rising. The congregation fell and rose, fell and rose.

This has to be God then, Michael John thought. *See how the people kneel and then rise. This is God showing himself to us and these people know that. This is just like the real Palm Sunday. This is the end of the world, it is so deep and so real.* All these thoughts flooded his brain with a rush so sensual and exciting that he felt himself lifting up. That was his call. *I want to be the one who brings this to the people, brings God to the people.*

Michael John, it seemed, had applied and already been accepted to St. John's College and Seminary in Brighton. He would begin his studies the Monday after Labor Day. He would not need black clothes as of yet. Freshmen were asked to wear jackets and ties. Once you became a sophomore in the college, you were required to wear black trousers, a black belt, a white shirt, a black tie. A jacket or a sweater were optional, but black was not optional.

Michael John went on about the clothing for some minutes while Jo's mind tried to make peace with his announcement. That his plan was already in motion was a fact that she took in and felt as a betrayal, an abandonment—but first and foremost, a judgment of her devoted attention to him. She tried to reconcile it to the promise she had made to their mother on her deathbed, that, yes, she would watch over Michael John. She had always known that promise would mean no marriage for herself, and she had sometimes wondered how his eventual marriage would affect her duties, but this scenario in front of her had stupidly not occurred to her. *Mother, do not worry*, her brain prayed, formulating *her* plan, all of this running in an undercurrent to her listening to him.

"I have heard the call, too, Michael John. It's the Mercies for me."

He looked at her with level eyes, taking her measure in a bold way she had never seen before. *I will be my own man*, his eyes signaled to her like flags from one ship to another in code. *I will be my own man.*

Meanwhile, Anne fell in love with Fred O'Brien who always played shortstop in the street baseball games. He was handsome and kind. They married the year Michael John was ordained, the same year Perpetua took her final vows. The three of them were committed by promises made to God, or, in Josephine's case, to Mother.

Final vows were sometimes called perpetual which meant not only eternal but continuous. You were entering into a situation where every moment tied back into what you had vowed however many years before. Every breath perpetually bonded. *Fiat*, be it done unto me.

For Anne, walking on her father's arm down the aisle—an aisle her father had designed—was wrenching and almost physically painful. The idea of leaving him, even leaving his name, and giving herself, her very body, over to this … this man … this Fred O'Brien, twisted her insides until she feared she would topple. She gripped her father's arm tighter.

"You are beautiful, my darling girl," he whispered as they walked, nodding ever so slightly to the assembled families and friends. "All I want is your happiness."

Nod, nod. her veil bobs up and down.

"And if he ever raises a hand, Anne Marie Cooney, if he ever …."

She squeezed his arm. "Now, now," she cooed from under her veil. But when her father handed her over to Freddy, her knees almost went. She felt a pain inside like a hunger pang, and a whirring in the back of her throat. But, when she felt Fred's hand in hers and looked into his kind eyes, she stopped shaking. "Now, now," she said to herself. "Now, now."

Orate, Fratres

ACT IV: Pray, brothers

SCENE I: The Chant

(Altar boys file in, in formation. They are dressed in cassocks and surplices. All but one of them has on polished shoes. They bow to the altar in unison and turn to face the congregation, forming a line behind the Communion rail. This is an unusual thing to do, and the congregation communicates its uneasiness through coughing and the scuffling of feet. As if a boys' choir, they chant.)

ALTAR BOYS:

✳It was not that Peter was born Catholic exactly. His mother, who had given him up for adoption, just believed in signs. She named him Peter, hoping a saint's name, a pope name, would be good luck. She hadn't let herself love him or his twin sister; she just wished them luck. The least you could do for a kid was a name... a name that would last him, a name with some promise, yes, with some luck.

Name him after a big saint and that might get him through life. She hadn't bothered to name the girl, though. Let the nuns do that.

ALTOS:

After the first orphanage closed, when Peter was about four, he ended up at a home for throwaway kids, the abused, runaway, orphaned kids. He wasn't really sure how old he was and had never bothered to check his records. The nuns at the new place assumed he was born Catholic. They had him blessing himself and dropping down on one knee before sitting in the pew in Chapel. They had him ringing the bells that chimed a noise like ice crystals whenever you merely touched them. They thought he was holy; they whispered of a vocation.

CONTRATENORS:

Sister Helen of the Holy Cross, as short and tiny as her name was long,

> (Sister Helen in full habit is lowered from the catwalk. Her hands are joined in prayer formation, her lips are moving, her eyes are closed.)

prayed for him special at the end of every Mass and at every noontime Angelus—

SOLO:

The angel of the Lord declared unto Mary/And she was conceived of the Holy Ghost.

RETURN TO UNISON:

That Peter might be the answer to her prayers for more vocations, for a vocation from their very own. One of theirs. Someone to come back to give them Holy Viaticum on their deathbeds and say sweet homilies at their funeral Masses. She prayed every Mass, every Angelus. For Peter.

> (Sister Helen slowly disappears into the rafters.)

As he got older, Peter loved to stand among the priestly vestments hanging in the sacristy closet. The satins, the smooth, solid colors—the purples, the ivories, the black so black it was dry, and the unchaste red, a reminder of sin and women. He even liked just opening the door to this cupboard. The skeleton key, poking out of its keyhole, worked like a handle to the narrow oak door. You pulled on it lightly, the door would break its seal with a soft puff, and there they hung, the dresses that priests wore for every Mass, changing colors with the season or with the holiness of the day.

All the priests and the sacristan nuns who took care of the altar cloths and the vestments knew which color the feast day called for.

(Altar boys look up to the rafters as if seeing Sister Helen again.)

Sister Helen of the Holy Cross knew; it was she who was responsible for coordinating the altar, the tabernacle, the cruet table, even the priest himself with just the right combination of satin and tassels and linen. With the rustle of satin and the hushed scrape of the pushing and pulling of the hugely wide but shallow drawers, which held all of the cloths like file drawers for blueprints, she'd find the necessary serviettes and covers exactly where she had put them.

Peter, eight years old, had just done his first confession and received his first Holy Communion, and he was learning how to be an altar boy— the highest honor a second grader could be chosen for. He absorbed the image before him, of the priest in the sacristy, behind the part of the sanctuary where the altar stood, preparing himself for Mass. The priest was dressed in a white nightgown, called an alb, and he bent a bobbing bend to kiss the thin ribbon-like stole he held before draping it around his neck. The man prayed in mumbled foreign syllables, all the while bowing; hands extended, he rubbed his forehead, his lips, his chest with his thumb as if erasing mistakes that had happened there. All this holiness would have gone unseen were it not for Peter, who kept his eyes downcast, "closeted," as the nuns said, lest the priest feel his privacy being violated and curtail Peter's privileged access to the scene.

It seemed to Peter the priest must truly believe, if he went through all of that ritual in such a perfect way before getting out there in front of the altar to actually say Mass. It were as if he believed the Mass would not work had he not kissed his stole and bowed and rubbed, hidden there back in the sacristy, beforehand. Belief like that was impressive.

(In hushed tones.)

Making sure he was alone, Peter would open the cabinet door making the soft puff sound when he pulled on the key. He would step in between the folds of the vestments, feeling their sleek skin, soft as a snake's back. He would rub that sleekness against his cheek, his eyes closed.

SOLO:

One time he kissed the red satin one, sucking a fold of it into his mouth, and it felt like a tongue.

RETURN TO UNISON:

The sweetness of the priests' vestments was nothing like the grainy coarseness of the nuns' black serge habits. The priests got to wear dresses and the nuns wore sackcloth. He would be a priest.

(Altar boys look up.)

You will have your priest, Sister Helen of the Holy Cross, you will have your priest.

(Altar boys turn and bow to the altar, and then exit in formation.)

The Secret

ACT V: Pray Silently

SCENE I: Seen One

(The priest recites silently one or more secret prayers.)

Father Michael John:

✳Ben, yes, I pray for Ben, wherever you are. Ben, all of them. Bless them. Thanks be to God for the skin of their bodies, for the pressure of their muscles under that skin, for the smell of them, for the fullness of their buttocks, for the tussle, the wrestle, first playful then raw then turning soft and full and warm.

Pray for the baby, the child I will never know, pray for the soul of her mother now dead.[5] Pray for my soul, for I killed her. Pray for my soul, for I ever only really wanted Ben after all. After all.

Angelo's supermarkets smell of Romano cheese. As soon as you walk in the door. They're modern stores, the doors slide open as you step near them, but there is this throw-back odor to the days when

---

5. When Anne received Communion from him that time at the cathedral and he had looked into her eyes and seen into her, she thought there was holiness in his eyes. Now, as she rubbed her beige-gloved hand guardedly on her tummy and frowned, she knew it what it was she had seen in his eyes: madness.

Angelo Sr. came off the boat and set up his first *groceria* on Plantation Street. Michelle Joanne didn't usually go to this Angelo's, she went to the one nearer Family House, but this one had that same smell.

She didn't undo her scarf because she'd only be a minute. It was early, no crowd. She went down the wrong aisle and came up another one and spotted him, her mother's childhood neighbor,[6] Father Michael John O'Sullivan. He'd been pointed out to her before, but they had never met. He was at the tuna, salmon, crabmeat end, and she was at the canned soup and sauces. She knew him right away, even from the back, because he had on that black cape he always wore that went clear down to his ankles. All the priests who studied seminary in Rome at North American Martyrs wore those capes; that's how you knew who the really smart ones were, the best ones, the ones they expected great things of.

He was on the right side of the aisle. He turned to the shelves, and as he reached, his cape fell back to his elbow. So, MJ saw it clearly as he fingered the can of crabmeat, slid his fingers around its bottom rim, and then with a quick move, pulled the can inside the cape. Under the cassock. Three cans disappeared this way. *This is a mistake*, she thought.

"Good morning, Father." An old lady came around the corner into the aisle then crashed her cart into his. "Oh, I'm so sorry!" she flustered. "Oh! Forgive me!" She bowed a little, bobbed is a better word. She worked her knobby hands around the tangle of carts.

---

6. When they were neighbors, Anne Cooney had adored Michael. He had even sketched her portrait once. The whole neighborhood had taken pride in his vocation, owned a piece of him just because of proximity. Perpetua, too, was prized, but she had always been stiffer and harder to champion. When he came back from Rome at about twenty-six years of age, Molly would say, "That Father Michael John has such a way about him." Molly called him Father the minute the ordination Mass was over. "You call him Father Michael John now," she would say to everyone around her. "He's earned it."

But Anne never had the opportunity to do so, because he was stationed in another parish, and she was wife and mother of a multiplying brood. She followed his story, though; she knew that he somehow was not becoming the success everyone had expected. And his sister, Josephine ... there was a tale she was found wading in Lake Quinsigamond in her full habit. She'd always seemed too intense.

"There, there, now, don't you get all a-dither," Father Michael John said. "Why, let's just say how nice it was we bumped into each other! Let's just say you never know what's around the corner! We could say you were going around the bend, but we won't, will we?"

He was talking too fast for the teasing and flirting he was doing. He freed the carts and then gripped her at the elbow and squeezed it a bit.

She looked up at him, into a face that must have seemed to her to be very young but was not young any longer, and said, "Get on with you, Father."

She pushed her cart down the aisle toward MJ who was trying to evaluate what it was exactly she had seen him do with the cans of crabmeat. The old lady caught MJ's eye. "Made my day!" She laughed and shrugged her shoulders. MJ nodded and smiled, and then she followed the priest, who had disappeared around the display at the end of the aisle.

Sanctus

(Holy, holy, holy)

✳"We say, "'There but for the grace of God go I.'" That's what we say when we see one," the orphanage nun explained when a Negro lady, large, in a lacy blue dress and white lacy collar walked by them on Main Street. She and her charges, the little girls from the home, were in front of the department store where the Yankee women always bought their gloves and slips. The girls had never seen a person whose skin was so dark. Joe Petrelli, the fruit man, had dark skin, but not like this lady's.

It was little Delia who sucked in her air first and then said, "Oh." Then she said out loud, worried, "What happened to her?" because she thought the lady had been burned to coal. The woman walked on by and perhaps did not hear Delia's exclamation.

"We say, 'There but for the grace of God go I,'" Sister said again and then went on to teach them—on that day and on others—her version of a lesson in what she called compassion. If you passed a cripple, a mongoloid idiot, anyone with a birthmark, or any Negro person, you were to say, "There but for the grace of God go I." The sister did not mention queer people, because no one said that word or even referred to that type of person; surely the grace of God had nothing to do with that. Sister did not mention the children born out of wedlock either, but she sometimes thought of that when she would gaze at her girls all lined up in uniform, ironed and shiny. That people were equal was what the nun thought she meant. "There but for" meant all people had been equal to start with in the eyes of God. But then some, once born, were graced with health, with white skin, with limbs that functioned and brains that calculated, with parents. Sister meant: Do not think you are any better than that colored lady is, because that could have been you born in that body, inside that skin. This was Sister's brand of democracy and compassion.

To Delia, however, it ended up meaning that it was all soup. God waved his hand over the face of the deep, deep soup and some sprang forth whole and some sprang forth hampered for life. It ended up being the soup itself that Delia thought about. When her own children, twenty years later, were in school in a postwar America that was feeling lucky and very much "there but for" indeed, she encouraged it when they bought Chinese babies.

The American kindergarten kids sent money to the Christian orphanages in China to take in the babies and feed them and clothe them. The kindergarten kids saved their pennies to save the babies. They were buying their lives and more importantly, their baptisms. Their eternal futures were in these five-year-old hands. If these kindergarteners did not save their coins and buy these babies out of their hillside unbaptized deaths, they were allowing them to be doomed for all eternity in Limbo which meant you never, never got to see God, which seemed a peculiarly horrible sentence for God to exact on little babies. But there it was, and the kindergarteners took this on very seriously and wholeheartedly.

Delia's daughter, Christine, saved every nickel, every penny, no lollipops, no popsicles. She had to choose at different points whether to buy a quarter of a baby for one dollar, or a half a baby for two dollars and not get to name it, or to refrain and save five dollars for the whole baby and the right to choose her name as well as save her.

You earned points and won prizes. The prizes were picked out from a catalog; would it be a plastic holy-water font with *IHS* painted on it in gold, which stood for *I Have Suffered*; or the rosaries in the see-through plastic pouch with *Pray for Us* written on it in white lettering; or, a picture of the Madonna with the Christ Child, small, medium or large, depending on the total number of points you had accrued?

For each Chinese baby purchased, the American child would also receive a document that was then tacked up above the blackboard in her kindergarten classroom. The document looked like a diploma, all parchment with scrolls of ink along its margins. It was official. It was signed by a monsignor and had a gold seal in the lower right hand corner. Somewhere on it would be inscribed the Christian name chosen for the baby. The buyer got to request a name, but the nuns or priests over in China had the final say. They could decide, for instance, that there were already too many Chinese Theresa's in a particular orphanage. So, they might substitute a less popular Christian name like Agatha or Helen. If there were a sole purchaser, that name appeared on the document, but if the purchaser were a whole class, then only a group name would be written in, such as Holy Redeemer Kindergarten. Then for sure, the orphanage got to pick the baby's name.

So if someone wanted a baby of her own with the name of her choice on the official document, a name like Delia, then that someone would have to come up with all the money herself. On the other hand, the kindergarten class *had* to buy them; they needed to. The babies these kids were buying would be otherwise left on Chinese hillsides to die. Especially girl babies and babies born out of wedlock. *(Dear girls, those Chinese don't want girl babies because they think girls are inferior to boys, but we do not think that. And of course, God does not think that.).* The Chinese people also put girl babies on the hillsides because girls would grow up to be mothers, and they were trying to control the number of people in their country *(and we don't believe in that either.)*

Delia's daughter, Christine, bought so many babies there were no prizes she had not earned. How many holy-water fonts did one family need? Delia wouldn't allow any more in the downstairs rooms, and Christine could sense that her parents were beginning to think it strange, so many holy-water fonts at every doorway. Christine used them all, each time she passed. She would dip the tips of the third and fourth fingers in and cross herself rapidly, holy drips flying as she'd sweep from one shoulder to the other.

Many years later, Delia's Christine, would hold in her arms the baby she would never have and let herself be named the baby's godmother at her baptism. She would stand between the baby's mother and father, holding her and repeating eerie words in echo to the priest's voice. Words about denouncing the Devil and about belief, words that she did not believe. What Christine did believe and stand up for was the beauty of this gorgeous infant. She believed in her breath, in the suction of her tiny nostrils, in the chafed rosiness of her cheeks, in the fall of the lashes of her eyes against her skin, in the miniscule flutter they made as she breathed, while sleeping. She believed in the beauty, the purity, the innocence, the wholeness, the divinity breathing in her arms, and she disavowed any hint that this infant would have sin on her soul; she eschewed, spat out, vomited any sense that this baby was originally blemished.

"Baby, bless me," Christine would say to this divinity in her arms. "Baptize me with your purity."

And she did.

Consecration

... in remembrance of me

＊Perpetua finds she cannot bring herself to teach transubstantiation any longer. Nor can she teach the Trinity. It is an unraveling.

No one else knows this. No one would ever question whether she were teaching transubstantiation and the Trinity. This is it: you do not assume that the stranger sitting across from you on the bus eats and urinates and defecates in order to live. You would never couch a sentence, "I assume that stranger urinates." Your attitude is more fundamental than that; it is more fundamental than assumption, than belief. You know this person eats and urinates and defecates, and it is not because you know the other person but because you know yourself and your human nature and you identify this other being as having the same nature as yourself.

She never taught either of these concepts any more because she had come to believe in a Trinity and a transubstantiation that encompassed the whole entire world. She would have said— had she admitted it, which she did not, not really even to herself—that she had come to believe that Niagara Falls, for example, was just as much a transubstantiation into the body and blood of Jesus Christ as was the wafer and the wine. She revealed to no one that she not only had a copy of Pierre Teihard de Chardin's *Divine Milieu*, but had committed it to memory. Her idea was that if all the books were destroyed in her lifetime, surely there would be some people who had memorized the Bible and some who had memorized Shakespeare so that life could go on. She would be the one who had memorized Teihard so that life could go on.

But what was, of course, truer was that she believed nothing. Not a bitter twit of it. She still kissed each piece of her clothing, her habit, as she dressed in the morning as she had been trained; she prayed all the prayers and she knew all the answers. But she had for so long not believed any of it that she could no longer remember when her conversion to nonbeliever had happened.

> (Spot up on platform suspended stage left. Blackboard behind him, a priest in his blacks faces audience and points to written material on the board using a long wooden pointer with a black rubber tip. He has no chalk dust on his suit at all. The black gabardine shines like silk. The student chairs and desks in front of him are empty. He lectures to the empty seats with great seriousness of purpose.)

PROFESSOR PRIEST:

First, as to the church's teaching on transubstantiation. At the Last Supper, Jesus took the bread and the wine, and he broke the bread and blessed it and said, "Take this and eat it for this is my body." In a similar manner he took the cup and, blessing it, gave it to them saying, "This is the cup of my blood, the blood of salvation, which is to be shed for you for the forgiveness of sins." And then, he said, "Do this in remembrance of me."

> ["Symbolizes vs. transubstantiates," the professor priest writes on the board.]

PROFESSOR PRIEST:

To the Roman Catholic, this Communion food only appears to be food. The true substance of the consecrated paper-thin wafer is flesh, and the true substance of the consecrated red wine is blood, and divinely so, because this is the flesh and blood of the one we believe to be God.

> [Spot out on Professor Priest. Spot up on Smoking Woman, who is now sitting atop a bar stool, a drink in one hand. Smoking Woman leans forward and addresses the audience.]

Perpetua did not believe that. She did not, either, believe in the Protestant watered-down version of a Last Supper symbol. Her theory was God = Energy = the Incarnate World, matter (Jesus) (M) times the Spirit of God (C) squared. The Trinity. Follow?

Perpetua couldn't teach this brand of trinitarianism or transubstantiation out loud because, first, it wasn't dogmatic, and second, her First Holy Communion class was not ready to understand such things, but, and most important, third, were she to express these beliefs, even as theories, they would ask her to leave. Ambrose herself would call her in, and wouldn't Ambrose be happy, too, and she would say, "It is clear to us, dear, that you are no longer in the fold of the Roman Catholic church and it is time for you, then, to leave this community of Sisters." Meanwhile thinking (Ambrose) that Perpetua was crazy, that only a crazy person could dream up such an odd belief, and that perhaps the brother, the priest, was just as whacko.

I will ask him someday, Perpetua thought, *I will ask him what he thinks his hands do.* Sister Mary Perpetua sat in the convent chapel and focused on the dust motes in the stream of sunlight beaming through the Paraclete's head, which hovered over Mary and the apostles in the Pentecost window. This was her cenacle, upper room, hideout.

I will say to him, "How is the believing of it different for you, since it is actually a matter of your own hands?"

She would have asked him before, but the rare Sunday afternoon visit to the graves never yielded the opportunity, and she feared he would think it strange, even heretical, of her to ask, indeed to think, such a thing. Her fingers were knotted in her twisted rosary. The little metal crucifix at the end cut into the palm of her hand as tightened and pressed it there. He was not talking to her any more. The nuns did not talk to her either. She had never expected them to, never wanted it; she'd discouraged it, in fact. She was the priest's sister, after all; she had a role, a place. But the silence seemed haunted these days. These days she felt herself floating in oblivion.

Sundays, once a season, he would pick her and a companion up in his car to go to the cemetery. Nuns could never travel unaccompanied by another sister even if it were their priest-brother who was doing the driving. The sisters would vie for Perpetua's companion duty. *To be in his presence is inspirational,* they would perhaps be thinking, to cover the deeper truth that to be in his presence was electric, a humming buzz of some energy that felt holy and ecstatic. prideful. The chosen companion would swell with pride to be with such a priest, to be seen with such a priest. To accompany the brother and sister—such a gift to

God, a siblings' double vocation—was a source of grace in itself. The companion would hang back so that the two could have their private time of prayer and respectful grieving. She would be most thoughtful.

So, Sundays, once a season, he would pick her and a companion up in his car to go to the cemetery. The two sisters would sit in the back seat of the car, and the brother, appearing the chauffeur, would drive slowly in his tank of a sedan, the priestly black Chevrolet model. The brother and sister would speak.

"Sleeping well, Father Michael John?" Perpetua would catch his eyes in the rearview mirror.

"Very well, Sister Perpetua, very well indeed."There was no "and you?" because such a question of a nun, even one's sister, was too carnal.

"We pray for you daily, Father, and for your parishioners."

Is this what they talk about? the companion wonders. She remembers her visits with her brothers and sisters, and stifles a smile at the memory of the jokes, the songs, the combustion.

"I will be transferred, Sister, perhaps you know that already."

"No," Perpetua paused. "I know nothing of that, Father Michael John. When and where?"

"At the usual time—August—and it seems I will be going to the cathedral, Sister."

Perpetua felt a flutter in her heart, a gush she had to disguise in her voice, a thrill: "Is it the cathedral then, Father?"

"Yes, I will take on curate duties, mostly hospital visits to the sick and the elderly. Beginning in August."

"I see." She lowered her eyes and was grateful that their companion this day was not of the political type to wonder why a curate's duties, why not a promotion. Was this a demotion? Did they want him under watchful eyes, therefore, the cathedral?

Perpetua did not understand at all. He was stellar, sterling, full of promise. Why hide him doing sickroom ministries? What could they be thinking?

"I shall speak to Mother General, Father."

"And that would be about—?"

"About effecting my own transfer to our convent on High Street next to the cathedral."

"That won't be necessary, Sister Mary Perpetua. But we will talk about it later." He suddenly became aware that the companion was paying close attention to the notion that Perpetua would approach Mother General.

Perpetua was not paying attention to her companion anymore. Her mind was flying along much faster than this funereal tank. *Get us there,* she thought. *Just get us there so I can talk to you alone.*

They approached the stone as they always did, side by side but separated by four, five feet. They walked toward it in a manner that was half self-conscious strolling and half sacred procession. The companion turned her back generously and stayed by the car, taking in the day's beauty, the sun glinting off the granite stones and the geraniums vivid and healthy against them.

He stood. She knelt. He reached into his pocket for his sterling silver rosaries that slipped and slid together in gentle rhythm, gentle rhythm, with each step he took. She took hold of the mammoth beads that hung from her belt. He led them, of course, and she returned, the phrases woven in and out in rapid shuttle.

"Why the cathedral? What is happening?" She stood, he closer to the stone than she.

He looked down at the stone and bent over to place his flat and open hand on the top edge, as if pressing it down, making sure it would not rise up.

"It isn't for us to know or to question."

"I know, I know, but what do you make of it?" She walked around the stone so he had to look at her.

"I am so tired, Jo, so tired. I cannot keep up. I—I—I don't want to make anything out of it. I am just going where I am told to go."

"Something is not right. You are not right. Tell me, tell me what it is." She couldn't let on to him she knew. She knew everything and she truly did not want him to tell her, not at all.

"If I could, I would."

Perpetua pushed the crown on her gamp up off her forehead a tiny bit baring the deep ridge permanently imprinted there. "I am getting to the convent down there, at the cathedral, down on High Street—"

"We've asked enough favors of your superior." He shook his head slowly.

"All I do for her, for them? These requests aren't favors, brother, they are our just due."

"Not how they look at it, Jo, not at all how they look at it."

"Is it that you are sad, Michael John? Mother would want you to confide in me."

And for the first time in years, he really looked at her. He reached out first one hand and then the other, and holding her hands over the grave of their mother and father he said, "There is nothing, nothing, anyone can do for me—not even you." He paused then for a long moment, while her heart throttled. "Time to go now," he said. "Time to go."

On the ride back, Father Michael John asked if they would like to hear some of the ball game. The poor, pitiful companion practically fell forward over the front seat in response. The nuns were only allowed to listen to the radio should war be declared. The car filled with the cracks of bats and the muffled roars of the Fenway crowd and the angular tinny sounds of the announcers' explanations. Stealing a base, sliding, and then the pitch, the call, the drumming of the plaintive "Ball one ...."

Whatever this transfer means, we'll make a good come-out of it. He will need me more than ever now. They must have the pastorship in mind for him, pastor of the cathedral. Getting the rich who have removed to the suburbs to support the central church of the diocese, that was the ticket. She knew how to play this game. How she knew, she wasn't at all sure, but her mother had known that she'd have enough savvy to figure things out for him. He was so naïve, so innocent. *Help me, Mother,* she thought, referring not to the Virgin Mother of God but to the one in the grave that they'd just left. Their mother would intercede with that other Mother who would intercede on their behalf.

"Grand slam!" Her companion bounced on the seat.

"Why don't I just drive once more around the block so we can hear the crowd, Sister, okay?

Did he wink just then? Had she caught him winking? Get me home. Time to get me home.

Prayers for the Dead

Memento etiam, domine,
famulorum famularumque tuarum, qui nos
praescesserunt.

(…those who have gone before us)

(A single white-painted iron bed sits in an infirmary room. Next to the bed is a simple wooden table, small, painted white, and set with a single gold candlestick and a free-standing crucifix atop a square linen cloth. A woman is in the bed. She moans, Her head drifts back and forth against the pillow. It is Perpetua. She has an unruffled white linen cap on her head, tied under her chin. A young woman, dressed all in white with a long skirt and veil, her wide sleeves hooked up to her shoulders revealing tightly fitted full-length sleeves underneath, which cover her arms. She is a nursing nun. Perpetua does not speak aloud, but we hear her.)

✳"Who is this girl? If only I knew her the way she knows me. I could match her then." Perpetua's hands fuss with the edge of the blanket, trembling, fussing. "Don't I mean master, not match? Master her the way it feels she is mastering me? How does she know before I know that I want the window closed, that I am thirsty and it must be lemonade, that it's time to … to whatever. How does she know these things? She has somehow memorized me without my taking notice of its happening. And now it is too late. She knows me now too well, so well that I will never escape her. So well, perhaps, I will even get to the point of not wanting to escape. That is how, surely, she anticipates me. She has broken my code when I did not even know I was communicating—not in any language, coded or not."

A cup of steaming tea has landed at Perpetua's elbow. It is perfectly rosy, perfectly sweetened. "Just what I want," she thinks, before she catches herself and realizes that this girl in white had done it again. "How does she know these things? And ... what else does she know?

Perpetua remembers Mother Ambrose, her superior, her mother general. Her salvation. "Before Mother died," Perpetua says as her head falls slowly to one side, her eyes floating as memory crowds out her pain. When Mother and she were the only ones who cared a twit whether either of them breathed or not, after Michael John had been found out, they were unified, Mother and Perpetua. Not even two peas in a pod but one pea—one rounded, symmetrical, no-beginning-no-end ball of wholeness.

"Then the bitch died on me." A shaft of pain—is it the memory or the cancer?—lards her brain. "They all die on me."

"Now what?" she thinks. The words *How could you?* pit the roof of her mouth like acid. "Die. Fine. Who said *you* could die? Bury me too, then, or, no need to. Sit me here and I will decay to crumb and disperse myself, thank you very much. Oh, thank *you*, Mother. Mo-o-o-ther Mary Am-bro-o-o-se, for abandoning me to do this dying on my own. Just sit me here."

Next thing Perpetua knows, windows are letting in a breeze. Toast comes on a plate. Her feet get propped up, kneaded.

"Ah. Who is this girl? Maureen she says she is. But, who is this Maureen?"

Perpetua closes her eyes, opening them to the memory inside. "Mother has died," she thinks. Yes, and maybe she thought her dying would kill me too, drown me to suffocation." A thought: "What would Perpetua eat without her?" Another thought: "Perpetua would soon become stench, too. This might have been Mother's plan all along.

"But if that were Mother General Mary Ambrose's plan, it would not work because of Maureen.

"Suddenly, afghans get tucked in around my thighs and pillows plumped. If you do not stop, I think (Or, do I say it out loud? Or did I scream it just then? Or merely think it?), if you do not stop, Maureen, I will never get dead. And I am to be with Mother. That is all there is. All there is to it."

It does not seem to matter what Perpetua thinks or feels, and it is not at all clear whether she is actually voicing herself. Life gets carried on about her, around her, for her, yet she cannot hear Maureen, only her own voice happening inside of herself. This is where suspicion comes in. "This, this, Maureen … has she kidnapped me? Does she hold me against my will? I do not know. Perpetua does not know."

The chanting happens and she recognizes it. It pulses inside her, a matter of pressure and valves more than belief or thought or praise. The chant is flesh and blood, the nuns' simple existence praising God. Chant *becomes* them. They do not *do* it, they do not *chant*. They *are* chant. A novice does not understand this at first, but soon understanding comes, and eventually even understanding it will slip beneath the surface and die. And then, then, *finally* a nun chants. She will be the chant.

"Mother. I placed my head below your hem. I asked for your foot to step over me. Step over me. I am your threshold."

"Find no honor in your humility," came the reply. "I take notice only of the maggots your flesh will draw to itself as I await your liberation from the tomb of your body. I do not step over you as much as my foot passes through you. You are of no moment. You are no threshold. You are simply beneath. Something a little more than nothing, but little, barely more.

"I only want for your eternal happiness in heaven. Today is as nothing. All shall pass away except the everlasting glory of God. I do not hear you. It is only a body that speaks. Draw into yourself until you are so small you are a mite, and then I will listen, then your voice will be powerful and will call me to my liberation."

On and on. Does Perpetua speak aloud? Can Maureen hear her? Can Mother hear her cries?

"I broke grand silence, forgive me," Perpetua thinks. "I coveted James Marie's oatmeal. Forgive me. I desired shoes that would fit my feet, a mattress that allowed me sleep. Forgive me, Mother.

"She is going to burn me alive, this Maureen," Perpetua thinks. "My suspicions were correct."

Maureen takes a candlestick, heavy and thick, and centers its square base solidly on the white linen cloth on the white table next to the white bed where Perpetua lies.

The candle is impossibly thick, yellowy-creamy white like long-ago remembered marzipan. Even its wick is thick. She lights another candle a little farther off. More candles. A ring of them around her bed.

"She will burn me alive. But how does she know that is exactly what I want her to do?"

What they all know but do not admit is that the chant can reach its throbbing point in an urgent almost painful flowering in one's pubis. If a nun can keep her eyes closed, keep the lids of her eyes from flying open in surprise, in delight, then she will get to go deeper and it will last longer, the flowering. None of them talks of it. None of them talks.

"Cleanse my heart and my lips, oh, almighty God, as thou didst cleanse the lips of the prophet Isaiah with burning coal." Priestly gospel words jostle her memory at the thought of being burned.

Maureen winds the rosary in and around Perpetua's clasped fingers. The beads are worn smooth to almost soft, the color of seeds. Perpetua's fingers are clasped. Clenched so, and so wrapped up by the beads, she wonders, "Am I manacled? Or, is this grace?"

Maureen seals her lips with an oil Perpetua cannot taste. She cannot scream. Maureen presses her patient's eyelids closed, places her thumb against the patient's forehead at the crease where the coif engraved its mark. Below her neck, Perpetua realizes, "I am no longer alive."

Maureen's hands are moving slowly about, perhaps pressing more oil into more places on Perpetua's body.

"Perhaps this Maureen girl does not know those parts of my body are dead now. Lost. Lost. But, she has known everything, so surely she knows that. Breath—is it mine?" Breath in a chanting fills her ears with a roar from inside her head, a seashell's inside ocean roaring. Only her neck and chin and cheekbones breathe. All the rest is dead.

"Mother …."

The Minor Elevation and the Our Father

Through him, with him, and in him

✳The week all of Christine's relatives died, her Auntie Gertrude, long senile, long lost, went first. It happened in the nursing home eight long years after she virtually died of drink and demented loneliness. Gertrude was buried by her brother Walter's parish, since she'd been so long gone from her own. Only a funeral Mass, no wake; the church, packed. The brother of Christine's deceased father and the brother's wife Tilly had many friends, and they turned out for the show, that is, the show of respect.

Christine sang at the funeral. She sang and wished self-absorbed and wistful thoughts about Auntie Gertrude and how she—Christine—could have done more. Gertrude had turned on Christine in a boozy state years before and in so doing had freed her niece from any sense of responsibility for her. But, she had loved her aunt once and thought her sophisticated and worldly. Christine sang and wished she'd done more.

They all went to lunch after the burial (a collation, they called it)—Uncle Walter and Aunt Tilly, a niece of Tilly's, and Tilly's sister Florence. The niece said, "Sit next to your Uncle Walter, Christine, you don't get to see him much." Christine felt judged by that remark, and she felt guilty because she did live only two hours away. She could see him more. In the opposite-side niece's voice, Christine heard what she had heard whenever these two niece-in-laws came together: "Walter is mine, really, but you can visit briefly."

Christine thought what she'd always thought: *You can think that, Miss Niece, but Uncle Walter and I know who we are to each other. I am the eight-by-twelve baby picture framed in sterling silver on his goddamned bureau, lady. That is who I am.*

But Christine just smiled and nodded, took the seat across from Uncle Walter, and watched him eat an open-faced steak sandwich. Just what her father, Walter, and Gertrude's oldest brother Jim Roy would have ordered.

Walter was dead the next morning. Tilly found him of course. She called Christine.

No. No. Two in two days? Impossible. Poor Tilly. What will she do?

She'll die. No, Tilly will make it through the wake and the funeral, and through Christine's singing the same hymns. She'll make it through the limo ride to the cemetery. She'll make it through the collation at her nephew's home. She will eat none of the doughnuts, none of the ham or the cheese. Then she'll die.

Tilly was the oldest of them at ninety-two, eight years older than her husband. She and Christine talked for a while over the soft clinks of coffee cups against their saucers and the whispering of stunned mourners commenting about the vagaries of life that would claim Gertrude and Walter, sister and brother, just two days apart.

Christine and Tilly had had a connection, always, because they had both experienced Gertrude's repudiation. Walter was Gertrude's baby brother and had lived with her until his forty-sixth birthday when he'd announced he was marrying. Marrying fifty-four-year-old Tilly Campbell. Gertrude's shock and fury was only dimmed over the decades, never extinguished. Walter—her baby brother—remained an embarrassment over her attention, while her brother Jim, Christine's father, by choice and temperament would not put up with being coddled or taken care of. Walter had been Gertrude's baby all right and had been supposed to companion her to her death. Enter Tilly's end.

Since she died last, all the money went to the niece on her side of the family. Just desserts.

The Kiss of Peace

May the peace of the Lord be always with you.

[Congregation stands, answers, "And also with you." All turn. Smoking Woman speaks: "You, you there, you, turn. Turn! Embrace each other. Touch. Shake hands at least. Peace, say. 'Peace.' Or, 'Peace be with you.' Smile. Look each other in the eyes for God's sake. I mean it for God's sake. In the eyes!"]

✳ Live parking. Ninety-three degrees. Fourth day of nineties in a row. MaryAnne waved her arm out the passenger's side window as if there were a breeze to be caught. And she waited, live parked.

The voice found recognition inside her brain first. She felt the bristling of the punch of that recognition, as if the voice had recognized *her* and not the other way around.

The consequence of the punch was the awareness of a name was being born; she could feel it crowning. The prickles along the edge where her hair met her forehead indicated how deeply important this was.

Then, the name surfaced behind her eyes on the same screen that his face registered through her optic nerve. There he was, she saw him, and ... the ... name ... Bill. Fa—ther Bill, the name stunned her eyes wider. The second punch hit, then, right at her heart and caused bristling there too. *Father Bill*, the words echoed inside her again. At first a rush of joy, a thrill. Her hand waved out the window as if to catch him.

Ten, perhaps fifteen, seconds had transpired.

The eyes, the squinty smiling eyes, and the nose and the mouth were his. It was Bill, Father Bill. The same. As if still young.

He was showing two frail men the town. To the smaller of the old men, he spoke loudly, shouted really—that was the voice that had found her. Kindly bending over to him, he said, "Jeans. Do you still have your collection of jeans?" Laughter. He was happy with himself that he'd pleased them by remembering this fact.

His skin was tan, as it had always seemed. He wore a khaki whaler's hat and top-sider loafers and khaki Bermuda shorts. And he wore a shirt that touched just the right note, matching the khaki and adding a gray stripe. He sauntered. He gestured, showing them this shop window and that, suggesting they cross the street, and mentioning why not get back to the car. Ever gallant, and casually so, the way the youngest in a family grows up to be, the one who never worries about money—that is the way he showed them the town.

The town was P-town, Provincetown, and that early in the day it did not yet belong to the queens and the trannies. At that hour, lesbian carpenters commandeered the place, shouldering their way through pedestrians to get to their work sites. Too, lovely gay men, yearning to be writers or painters, cycled past to get to their waiters' jobs in time for the lunch rush. And busses offloaded senior tourists to pan through the shops.

Father Bill was showing it all to them, and *they*, the two frail ones, were clearly a couple. A couple of celibate retired priests, perhaps, virgins even, but a couple. They shared the same gait, the same taste in clothes and hats. They had the same librarian-white skin and rabbit eyes. It might have been fear coming off them like a scent, or, it could have been shyness, simply. Had they been Bill's teachers once? Could they be that old? Or, were they priests he had met on trips to Rome? Order priests, perhaps, Franciscans or Salesians. They were too innocent and weak to be Jesuits, too retiring to be Dominicans.

Kind. He could be so kind. And people loved him when they loved him.

When was it I saw him last? His mother's funeral—and they hadn't let him say the Mass.

Lord, I Am Not Worthy

(Domine, non sum dignus)

✳James J. Roy and his second wife, Delia, bathed once a week on Saturday nights, to be clean for church. It was private—surreptitious—perhaps because in their youth bathing meant the huge metal tub in the middle of the kitchen, filled with kettlefuls of heated water, soon scummy with repeated use.

Toward the end of Lawrence Welk, Mrs. Roy would slip out and twenty minutes later return scented and rosy, her feet puffy. That was the only time she was ever seen in her bathrobe, unless someone got sick in the night. Neither Mr. nor Mrs. Roy believed you should be in your bathrobe at any time not associated with your bath. And besides, being in sleeping clothes in front of your child was indecent. (After years of living in the same house, Christine, their only child, did not know if her father preferred showers to baths or even exactly when he cleaned himself. Bathing was shrouded, as was her parents' sexual intercourse, which she had come to believe must have happened only once.)

Her mother claimed that bathing during the menstrual cycle risked life-threatening contamination. So, depending on when your period came in relation to a Saturday night, it could be a long time between baths. You also wore your clothes as many days in a row as it took to get them dirty. That made sense, surely.

Christine wore her first-day-of-high-school dress again the second day, because the first week was half days, and she hadn't even begun to get it dirty in just one half of a day. Allana O'Toole pulled her aside. They knew each other vaguely; Allana's cousins lived on Christine's street.

"You can't wear the same dress two days in a row."

"What do you mean? It's not dirty." But suddenly Christine did know; she knew instantly what Allana meant. Why hadn't she realized it sooner? She could feel the layers inside her skin getting hot. Her chest was all strawberries. She swallowed. The heat was drying her out.

"People don't do that," Allana said. "We're in high school now."

There was no defense. Christine would never let it happen again. But it did, in a way, just once more.

Sister Geraldine of the Bleeding Heart of Jesus was an almighty bitch, through and through. Her front teeth appeared to be so white that they were almost blue, but the blue was because they were backed with metal. When she stood right next to your desk and talked to the rest of the class, if you leaned just right, you could see the roof of her mouth and all the metal on the back of her teeth. Her skin pulled squeaky clean over high, bright, pink cheeks. Tightly woven spider's web wrinkles connected everything on her face. It made you figure she was merry, but she was not merry.

She was German/Irish, about which she reminded the girls almost every day. "The very best combination, girls; good luck for you if that is what you are. The Germans, you see, are extremely intelligent, quick-witted, immaculately clean, and mathematically inclined as a people. The Irish are artistic, musical, and sensitive of spirit. Being a combination of both, I am doubly blessed. And so are you, no doubt, if that is what you are. What are you, ah, Marybeth?" And she began her roll call and went around the room. "Italian. Oh. I see. And … Kathleen? Irish, I suppose?"

Allana approached Geraldine one day, marched right up to her desk, and asked if she could have a word. A very adult thing for a freshman to do. Geraldine lost her rhythm, but only for a moment, and it was barely perceptible. Her left eye twitched the way it did when she realized she had the wrong answer in her book. Allana leaned down to whisper. "Sister, I think you should know that some people in this class do not bathe every day." Allana waited for that to sink in. "In fact, I know it for a fact that some girls only bathe once a week."

"Who?"

"I couldn't say, Sister," Allana looked down, suddenly demure.

"Yes, very well." Geraldine always preferred ferreting out the guilty herself. It was more of a challenge accusing the entire group and slowly, slowly, but painstakingly surely, weeding out the culprit. She usually managed to learn more names than the original tattletales knew anyway, and she always landed one or two who confessed to something they had not done. She enjoyed those particularly.

"I'll take care of it. Thank you, uh ... Allana." She paused in a way calculated to remind Allana just who was the student and who was in control. She didn't give Allana the grace period with which she usually awarded tattletales in order to diffuse the association between tattling and the lecture. Allana was getting uppity.

"Girls," she plunged right in, betraying Allana. "I am shocked, simply shocked, to learn something." As she continued, her eyes moved up and down each row. "I can't tell you how I look forward every night to drawing my bath."

The picture was difficult to conjure: The convent, the nuns all lined up in linen bonnets (because they were not allowed to see each other's shaved heads). Geraldine would be getting pinker and steamier. The spigots and faucets, the old-fashioned kind with heavy, shiny chrome. The fat overgrown lion of a tub, hard to swing into, hard to get out of. Couldn't quite get the clothes off of Geraldine in your imagination. The back of her teeth was intimate enough, thank you very much.

"But girls—once a week?"

The girls' odors were becoming more pronounced with each syllable. Allana, by now, looked chastened. What had she hoped to accomplish? One girl did smell, but it wasn't because she didn't bathe but because her mother thought deodorant was too grown-up for her.

"The Germans are a very clean people, girls. It is said they are the very cleanest people in the world. I am just glad that this was brought to my attention. For your assignment, write a five-hundred-word essay on the topic "Cleanliness is Next to Godliness" and copy it over three times.

After dinner, the dishes pushed aside, James J. Roy would lob his ham of a foot, red and naked, onto the kitchen table. Delia would roll up his trouser cuff and then get up to find her reading glasses and her clippers, the ointment and the powder. He would slouch deeper in the vinyl-covered chair.

They were primitive, his feet. The very definition of atavistic. The nails, hard as horns and ridged like clamshells, were yellow and curved almost over the tops of his toes. The toes themselves were chalky, like tiny granite tombstones, with lumps and red, juicing gashes festering between them.

"Ointment feels good?"

"Smells."

Silence.

"Get that corner," He said, pointing from his slouch, his nose and mouth gathered in disgust as if drawn together by a string.

"This?"

"Yeah," he sighs. "Hurt today."

"D'ya think them pads?"

"Listen, I don't know," he said, exasperation, not annoyance, in his tone. "I says to Bobby Kelly today, I says, 'Bobby, waddya' do with yer ath-a-lete's foot?' And he says to me, 'Jimmy,' he says, 'there's nothin' to be done.' That's what he says to me."

Christine heard it all from where she sat in her bedroom. Underneath the blooms of her breasts she felt a yell building, a please-stop-talking-about-puss yell or a what-does-Bobby-Kelly-know-about-anything-anyway yell.

But yelling would be foolish and Christine was too serious for that.

Communion

Jesus, Jesus, come to me
All my longing is for Thee
Of all friends the best Thou art
Make of me Thy counterpart.(Traditional hymn)

✳There was reason not to call it a wedding; there were several reasons. The primary one was that they had already been together in a loving, faithfully committed relationship for over two years. Another was that technically, legally, semantically, "wedding" meant the union of a man and a woman, even in the state of Massachusetts in the year 1998.

In 1998, to call it a wedding would be to pretend. And there was to be no pretense whatsoever attached to this celebration. Devise a new and appropriate name, if you would, but do not call it a wedding or a marriage until to do so would be true and recognized throughout the states. To make-believe would gloss over injustice. This day was not to be about gloss. This day was to be real, as real as breathing.

And there was the other reason, the one that meant the most to them personally. They did not wish to offend anyone. They way they loved each other and their friends and their family was founded on the deepest respect. They wished to be accepted as the people they were, neither icons nor, God forbid, stereotypes, and they wished to accept the love of their friends and family without any political litmus test. *Just love us*, they seemed to be saying. *You do not have to accept marriage between same-sex couples. Just love us. You do not have to stamp your approval on a revolution that will transform society. Just love us. The two people we are, the life we share. Once you love us and see how we love each other, you might be inspired in your own love relationships, which you call marriages, and you might come to understand such difference as there is, is not much of a difference at all.*

The invitation was shiny black, edged with gold; the parchment, pure white.

> "Join us to celebrate our years together and our commitment to many years to come. Join us, Christine Roy and Michelle Joanne O'Brien, in a ceremony of worship and communion, a prayerful honoring of how our lives have been blessed by God and by the love of our friends and our families. Join us."

They stood on either side of the massive front doors of the largest Unitarian church in town to greet each arriving guest. They stood at the head of the granite steps, which had been quarried in Quincy and hauled to this spot on a hill in the City of Seven Hills. Mayors had worshipped in this church and listened to the Fisk organ; freed slaves and Harvard College professors and physicians trained at Massachusetts General Hospital; even Presidents had walked these very steps where, this day, Christine and MJ stood in their finest clothes to greet each arrival with an embrace.

> (Sister Mary Perpetua and her catechism class enter stage right and process to the center, where they turn and begin to climb the historic granite stairs. The children, their hands folded in prayer style, move in solemn rhythm. They are dressed in the white suits and the bride-like dresses, the white shoes and socks of First Holy Communicants. Some of the boys wear veils, and some of the girls wear ties.)

> PERPETUA (shrieking):

This is not the church. This is not the right church at all.

> (The children kneel on the historic granite steps, forming two lines. Christine and MJ stand at the head of these lines at the front doors of the church. A woman dressed in clerical ceremonial robes descends from the platform above the stage. She sits in a rope/sling chair.)

CLERGY WOMAN:

Good morning on this beautiful day. I am Reverend Judith. I welcome you to this historic church and to this historic day in the lives of MJ and Christine. Let us pray: Oh, God, who grants us life and love, accept our thanks this day of celebration for the lives and love of MJ and Christine. Their commitment inspires us; their fidelity strengthens us; their joy propels us forward to sing your praises. I welcome you to come forward to receive the Communion of this church. We have a rule, and our rule is this: all are welcome to receive the bread and the wine of this sacred table. Come and receive if you believe this is the body and blood of the Christ; come and receive even if you do not believe this is the sacrament Jesus instituted two thousand years ago, even if you do not believe in Jesus or in the existence of God. Come if you want to share in this as a symbol of the love between MJ and Christine. This is the rule: all are welcomed to this banquet with love.

(Spot up on Sister Mary Perpetua, standing alone on center stage.)

PERPETUA:

When does this get to be my story and not his? When does my life get to be my life and not the life my mother expected of me? When does the sacramental grace that was to be my pension bestow its balm? I dream of sleep. Dream of it. Feel it like a jellied fluid spilling from a ruptured sac within my body, filling me, filling me, filling me with sleep. I could lay my head down right now, and I would not drift to sleep; I would sink to sleep, my consciousness a heavy weight urging my descent.

(Spot up on Perpetua's biological mother, who appears above, stage left, in her deathbed. Spot dims on Perpetua.)

PERPETUA'S BIOLOGICAL MOTHER:

She was always the queen of drama. Sarah Heartburn we called her; we called her that until it made her cry. He was quiet, off to himself always.

(Spot up on Father Michael John, who appears above, stage right, in a pulpit. Spot dims on the mother.)

MICHAEL JOHN:

This is the word: let me be. I am not even addressing the message to you, Mother, or you, Sister; no, this line is directly for the Big G-O-D. Let me be.

> (Michael John presses his hands onto the book splayed open in front of him on the pulpit—as if pressing it to keep it down.)

A friend of mine, a vowed religious as they are preferably referred to nowadays instead of "nun," which has a specific canonical meaning that truly does not apply to most of them, this friend of mine wishes that reporters and playwrights and screenwriters would describe sisters and priests as they really are. "Why don't they show our compassion and our sacrifices?" she asks me and laughs a little, nervous. She knows that she shouldn't weigh in on the outcome of artistic works in progress, but still, she says, "Tell the whole story," and shakes her head. "Not the Mother Teresa stuff, either, but the day-to-day, I-work-in-a-homeless-shelter kind of stuff, the modeling-my-life-after-the-Gospel-and-Jesus kind of stuff. I try to live a life of love," my friend says.

> (Father Michael John looks out to the congregation for a moment's pause, and then he pushes himself back from the pulpit as if from a feast where he has been overindulgent and is now disgusted by his excess. He turns and, looking sideways at the assembly, lifts his right hand and forms a cross in the air with a vertical and then horizontal sweep, blessing them. When he speaks again, he almost intones.)

MICHAEL JOHN:

Horrendous have been the sins committed by the clergy, oh Lord, but your grace has poured out through us, as well.

> (His voice changes to an ordinary pitch and he talks to the people now, not preaching, not blessing.)

Tell the whole story, people, tell it all.

Post Communion

✳The last time Delia Roy saw her husband was noontime five days before he died. After that day, she hadn't gone up to see him because she hadn't felt well. *Sickish. All the worry and the running back and forth. I have to keep up my strength,* she thought. She meant for the funeral.

Her only child, Christine, called to tell her he had died. Delia stared straight out of her eyes, then, after she hung up the phone—stringing out the look, unseeing, unhearing, a thread of a look, the spool gone wild. And unremembering, she hung there, where there were no anniversaries and there was no beginning. The surface of her eyes grew cool, and then cold, so she closed them, her first blink, sticky and dry over the cold surface.[7]

Delia won't know it for months—that she will love him finally now that he is dead. That she will love him with a heat that goes liquid in her dry place. One day, when she no longer wads up soft tissue to stop up her hole, but chooses tissue paper instead, because it is crisp and cuts through the warm syrup instead of absorbing it, she will realize that she loves him. She will realize it as she exchanges one tissue-paper wad, crisp and abrasive, for a fresh one and enjoys the exchange, and that will be the beginning of her rescue. As she sits up in bed reading—a pursuit which had held no interest for her before his death—the flow

---

7. Once at Christmas time, as a child, she had stuck out her tongue to ring the doorbell at the orphanage that she called home, and her tongue had frozen to it. Finally, when the portress pulled her free, part of the skin of her tongue remained there.

will come. The scene in chapter four is at first only provocative, then openly sexual.

"John pulls at her blouse with both hands," she reads. "With a cry that is small like an animal's, her breasts tumble out and away from each other, melons falling, the fruit basket ripped. He lunges for one with his mouth, the other he grabs with his hand, pulling and pushing on its fullness. His mouth takes her in and releases her in small, urgent swallows until her nipple is a tiny thing with its own urgency that he can feel against the roof of his mouth, against his tongue."

She will shift her buttock and feel her halves contract, her genitalia, grooved and hemispheric, a walnut of cramping energy. She will tighten her breasts and feel their points against her nightgown and with, no moan, she will pull the pillow high and tight between her thighs, and rock in little rubbing motions, at first still reading.

"Jessica begins to moan, her head back, her chin thrust away from him. She starts to move in deep circling thrusts, her hands finding him stiff and waiting for her...."

The pillow will not be enough. She will take the book, then, its hard covers shut, and she will put it down between her thighs, its binding rubbing stiff and hard against her tiny, red folded place. Rubbing, her thighs working, her hands, each at a breast, in rhythmic wonder, her tongue behind her teeth, on her lips, alive. Her mouth will gasp for a pillow to bite on, the rhythm coming harder. Never before like this. She will think of the pillow as her husband; he will have no face but he will, finally, know her. Soon, she will remember their lovemaking as if it had been this, and she will think she honors his memory whenever she repeats these motions. Once a night. Sometimes twice. She will feel the heat and call it love, and that will last her.

Final Blessing

ACT VI: Ite Missa est

SCENE I: (Go, the Mass is ended)

✳ There is a moment after receiving Holy Communion when a believer can be so full, so in thrall, so lifted, that she wants the Mass to be over and at the same time never to end. In Medieval times, each cathedral had a huge thurifer, an incensor that hung from the ceiling like a chandelier. It was some monk's job to pull its ropes, as if ringing a church bell, until it swung the full length of the church, dispersing incense in clouds like a crop duster. It was medicinal, really, more than liturgical. It was hoped that the incense would protect the congregation from the hidden specter of the plague.

In dreams, Perpetua had ridden such a thurifer like a trapeze artist flying high and graceful above the masses. Each time she raced through a swoop, her veil would catch the breeze and she would be aware only of the exaltation behind her breastbone.

> (An altar boy lifts a hand-held thurifer off its brass stand, which looks like a stand for a set of fireplace tools in a suburban den. He bends to one knee and adjusts the thurifer, which resembles a grandmother's sterling silver pepper shaker, only much larger. The thurifer has a filigreed, cone-shaped top that lifts off and slides along the chains that hang it from its holder. The altar boy swings it with these chains once he has started the chunk of charcoal

burning and dusted it with granules of incense that he has scooped up from the matching gravy-boat incense holder with its tiny silver spoon, until enough scented smoke has thickened to warrant closing the cone-shaped top, standing up, and, getting the feel of the chains in his hands, beginning the rhythm of the process: two small blips of swings in toward his torso, one wide swing out. The altar boy incenses the space.)

1910

Molly has not moved from her position in the eighth pew for the duration of the Mass. "Naimathafatha," she had begun, even before the priest had entered the sanctuary. Taking a swipe of a sign of the cross, she began, "Naimathafatha....

"I believe in God, the Father Almighty, Creator of Heaven and Earth—" she always began the rosary the traditional way with the Apostles' Creed, began it as soon as her knees hit the kneeler, before the priest had even appeared to say Mass. She began it with the reference to God the Father Almighty, but the rest of the rosary was safely about Mary, the Blessed Virgin, the Mother of God.

Molly prayed on blue glass beads, the blue reminding her of the Virgin. But rosaries came in all sizes and prices: pure gold, lapis, Murano glass, Barbarian crystal, knotted string, seeds, stones, shells, colored glass, pearls, gems, plain or glow-in-the-dark plastic, sterling silver, silver plate, base metal, wood, uncarved, and carved (some intricately like rosettes). The ones the nuns wore as part of their habit were five feet long, with beads as big as knuckles. They looped them around their belts in just such a way that when they walked, the beads rattled against their legs warning of their approach.

It was not supposed to matter what the rosary beads looked like or were made of. It was not supposed to matter if they had been blessed by the pope or were made from seeds from an olive tree from the Holy Land. But it did matter, of course. People did care, and much sinful pride was taken in owning eighteen-carat-gold beads blessed by His Eminence. If you counted on your fingers to keep track of the decades, you could pray just as well, because it was the prayer that mattered, not the expense or the beauty of the beads. But no one remembered that.

(Spots come up on various platforms suspended at different heights upon which rosaries are being prayed. A priest kneels.

A woman with an apron gazes off, washing dishes; a group of little children kneel by a bed; an old lady sits in a chair by a window.)

Pray each prayer as if each word counted; do not zip through in a torrent of gibberish. Do get into a zone, however, a drone of chant, where prayer is released from the simple meaning of the words and forms a meditative web. Say the Joyful Mysteries on Mondays and Thursdays. The first decade is the Annunciation. Picture the angel Gabriel flying into the room where Mary was praying. Remember that Mary is not praying the rosary, although that is how you want to picture her. Remember that Mary was just a teenager then. Do not dwell on your shock that she became pregnant at perhaps only thirteen but, rather, keep in mind that things happened differently back then. When Mary said, *"Fiat,"* that meant the Holy Ghost could impregnate her and it would not be a scandal that she wasn't married because she was engaged to a man named Joseph, a most chaste spouse, and if you were engaged back then, you were allowed to do it so everyone would just assume Joseph were the father.

Except Joseph.

Given Mary's purity and young age and, no doubt, cloistered existence, Joseph must have been totally undone by the pregnancy revelation, but picture his having a dream where an angel explains it all to him so, of course, he marries Mary, but never, ever, touches her in any way.

That is just the first of five decades in a series of three (Joyful, Sorrowful, Glorious). So that is just ten beads' worth, forty more to go for this round.

Molly Donoghue did not picture anything at all when she prayed the rosary. She had never "learned how" to pray it; she just had always prayed it, every day, when the family gathered before bed back in Cowskeep. The experience of praying the rosary was, for Molly, all about the words "thy womb, Jesus." You bowed your head at that point and paused, and a magic tug happened to you at that moment, every time. So familiar were the words inside the walls of her skin that they must have been etched with them, like bones surely make an impression on the inside of your skin, or like your brain must make on the inside of your cranium. These words, rumbling around inside her skull, inside her body, so often rumbling, surely they had etched themselves onto the interior walls of the shell that was her. The flow of words skidded to that heart-wrenching pause at "thy womb, Jesus." It felt as though Jesus were not so much the fruit of Mary's womb, per the actual wording and punctuation of the prayer, but was Mary's womb itself. "Thy womb Jesus."

Molly never took Communion. She believed she had sinned in ways the church could not forgive. Even though what George had done to her to make her pregnant was against her will, there was no forgiveness in it for her. There was no forgiveness that George was a Protestant and she had chosen him, what with her brothers dying the deaths they did, and all for what? So Ireland could be destitute and unified instead of destitute and partitioned? That mattered? No forgiveness meant no Communion, so no Communion for Molly, not only because she had sinned with a Protestant, the likes of which had killed her brothers, but also because she had hated them—George included—with all her heart, for which she had no remorse. And, indeed, had she stayed in Ireland, who knows whom she herself might have killed. Her rosary-drone during Mass was her buffer against the aching loneliness of spending a lifetime separated from her country, from her family, and from her one true love thywombJesus in the Blessed Sacrament of Holy Communion. What she could claim for all eternity was that she had done right by her babies, her twins.

Molly was slow to leave once Mass ended, whether she had come to the end of her beads in synchrony with the end of the Mass or not. If she finished them early, she still stayed until the Mass ended, the final blessing given. She stayed if there were a hymn, there usually was not, but sometimes. And even then, she would be slow to leave because for almost an hour before that, her position would have been a half-seated crouching kneel, her knobby hands crouched, too, bent around beads. So her body would rise slowly and stiffly, and as she would stand, she'd direct her attention from the side altar, where Mary's statue reigned, to the main altar and its central cubbyhole, the golden tabernacle. She stood, open, face fronted to this holy of holies, straight and unbowed. *I have done what I have done, the rest will be up to you.* She edged herself out of the eighth pew and, once in the aisle, gripped the pew's edge and bowed slightly in painful genuflection. *The rest will be up to you.*

1955

Anne O'Brien rose for the final hymn, "Holy God We Praise Thy Name," which was most often used at the closing. Some Sundays the Boy Scouts would carry the American and diocesan flags down the middle aisle, some Sundays, the Knights of Columbus marched. The Ladies Guild had another Sunday, when they would head downstairs afterward for a Communion breakfast, in which they broke their fasts with scrambled eggs and doughnuts and heard a talk by a visiting priest. Some Sundays, Sodality would leave in procession, or the St. Vincent de Paul Society. As they would pass her in the eighth pew, she would put on her beige gloves, neat and tight, as if applying them. She would nod and smile, recognizing faces as they marched by. She knew the words of the hymn, of course, so she would join in with the choir softy, very softy, " ... we bow before thee ... " She would genuflect but only down to the kneeler in the pew, not down to the floor of the middle aisle because the middle aisle was dirty and she could easily get a run. God understood. She would turn sideways and dip her knee down to the kneeler and quick bow her head, and, popping up, resume the final words of the verse.

Done. Another week done. Some people thought of the Sunday Mass as the beginning of their week. For Anne, it was the opposite. Mass was the culmination, which meant she had made it through another, yet again. *Deo gratias.*

Fred always stayed home to mind all the children, still too young to attend, so she had to get home to relieve him and allow him to get to his Mass. She always knew to avoid the bottleneck at the vestibule where the flags or the Sodality sashes or the Knights' sabers were being clanked and bumped and handed in. She would slip out the side door.

Today, she could feel the rim of nausea tightening in her stomach and she put her hand against her forty-five-year-old waist, hurrying down the stairs to the sidewalk, wondering if it would be a girl. How she wanted a girl this time. God never sent you more than you could handle, no cross you could not bear. Nine children and four miscarriages in eighteen years of marriage.

Saying the Mass, had Father Michael John noticed she was showing a little? He had blessed her and this gift from God at her request in the confessional last week, had told her she was doing God's work and not to be afraid. God never sends us what we cannot bear. She had rubbed her stomach with her gloved hand, then, and remembered the madness in his voice.

2000

MJ had not made it in time, and it haunted her. She was shredded with if-only-this's and if-only-that's, but strangely only about the priest—not about the fight between Jambo and that new resident and not about how she'd stayed in the bedroom without a worry, waiting for a Christine who would never come back to her. It was only the priest who haunted her. She had meant to get out to Lunenberg to visit him or to call. Seeing him in Angelo's had been a shock, but instead of the shock propelling her to move toward him, track him down, talk to him, check on him, it slowed her down and finally, like sludge in a pipe, wedged her to a stop. She had not written him. She had not called.

But she didn't stop thinking about him, about the way he swept those cans of crabmeat under his cape and about all the stories her cousins would tell her about this priest and their mom as kids in the old neighborhood.

He'd been missing for a few days before anyone realized. A priest alone, a tiny parish, a tiny community, gone off for a few days' rest, they might have thought, had they even noticed his absence. It was the howling of a dog that gave it away, gave him up to be found—at the Lunenberg fairground, an old amusement park, long abandoned and decaying. Any piece of equipment with an engine had been dismantled and sold off long before. The carousel had gone in an auction to a fair in Florida. Only buildings remained, boarded up and tipping lopsided.

Of course it would have to be that they found him in the Fun House, where the mirrors expose you to yourself in oblique ways, distorted. No one at the auctions had ever bid on those mirrors, so they stood there, mirrors opposite mirrors, reflecting multiple realities for an infinity of time. There was no note, so there would be no knowing the full story. As if there were ever a knowing of the full story.

MJ had not stayed until the *Ite Missa Est*. She had stood and faced the bishop when he said to the gathered seminary graduates on this, their special day, "Let those who wish to be ordained come forward."

She stood.

She sidestepped along the eighth pew and, reaching the middle aisle, stepped to the midpoint of the aisle and turned with deliberation to the altar. She took three strides forward, answering his call. Then she stood and faced him, this Bythabuk, this Bishop Peter Donoghue, ninety-year-old emeritus, the one who had seen it all. He held her look, his eyes dimmed with resigned patience, and his mouth grimaced sorrowful disapproval as if clucking, *tsk-tsk*ing.

Michelle Joanne turned her back on him and walked down and out the aisle, letting the heels of her pumps make spiking, echoing taps against the marble floor as she went, punctuating her departure. There was no way to slam the door as she left for good; the doors to the cathedral were too heavy and thick, too dumb to slam. Their immense weight could only be swung slowly away like the stone of the tomb. She swung herself out and around the door by leveraging her body against the huge wrought iron handle. Then, as though swinging herself off a train—or the way Ski could hop from the porch to the front yard—she jumped free of the handle and landed lightly on the granite floor of the portico. Free.

She breathed deep. "Air," she spoke to the air. "Air, we are going home." She was on the path to Family House where Barbara and Jambo were waiting. Where supper would be on the table. Where they would know her, know her in the breaking of that bread.

Appendix A

The Last Gospel

In the beginning was the word and the word was made flesh. (John)

Molly begat twins: Bishop Bythebuk and Delia.
Delia and James J. Roy married and begat Christine.
Josephine (Sr. Perpetua) and Fr. Michael John were brother and sister.
Anne, whose nanny was Molly, was a childhood friend of Josephine
and Michael John.
Anne married Fred O'Brien and begat many children.
Anne and Father Michael John begat Michelle ("M.J."). Anne died in
that childbirth.
Michelle married and divorced Leonard.
Michelle and Christine
married.
Christine died,
fatally
wounded at Family House.
Father Bill and Father Jim and MaryAnne were childhood friends.
Maureen, who once had been in Sr. Mary Perpetua's catechism class,
became a nun.